Torch Lake Summers
Growing Up at Camp Hayo-Went-Ha

Copyright © 2019 by R. Craig Hupp
Updated
All rights reserved

Author – R. Craig Hupp
Publisher – R. Craig Hupp
Illustrator – Rob Wilkinson
Cover Photograph – Rose Bechtold
Cover Design and Layout – Jeanette Gillespie

ISBN-13:978-1-7323967-0-8 – Print

Some of the characters and events in this memoir are fictional.

Proceeds from the sale of this book are donated to Camps Hayo-Went-Ha and Arbutus for camper scholarships.

Author

Craig Hupp is a retired lawyer and part-time resident of Torch Lake, Michigan. Craig is married to Ginger Keena– a quilt and costume artist – and has three daughters and five grandchildren. His writing efforts are supervised by his cat Tai Tai from her pad on the corner of his desk. *Torch Lake Summers* follows his father-in-law as he grows up as a camper and counselor at Camp Hayo-Went-Ha. Follow Craig's activities on www.facebook.com/craighuppauthor and at www.craighupp.com.

For a FREE Hayo-Went-Ha story, visit, https://craighupp.com/free-hayo-went-ha-story/

Illustrator

Rob Wilkinson is an artist and illustrator living in Whitley Bay, UK. He spent 15 years as a counselor and program director at Hayo-Went-Ha. He lives with his wife Jane (also a camp alumnus), sons Samuel and Elijah, and two cats, Lego and Brick. He can be contacted at rwrobwilko@gmail.com or through his Facebook page 'Rob Wilkinson Art' or Instragram at 'rob wilkinson art.'

Graphic Designer

Jeanette Gillespie started as a freelance graphic designer fresh out of college. She has worked with clients across the United States representing many different markets and platforms. Jeanette is passionate about health and fitness, being outdoors, great design, and real estate. She resides in North Michigan with her husband and family. You can follow Jeanette's adventures at www.facebook.com/jeanettekuzmagillespie.

YMCA Camp Hayo-Went-Ha
for Boys (Central Lake, MI) and Arbutus for Girls (Traverse City, MI)

The State YMCA of Michigan established Camp Hayo-Went-Ha for boys in 1904 and sister camp for girls, YMCA Camp Arbutus Hayo-Went-Ha, in 1996.

The State YMCA of Michigan provides programs for youth, teens, and families which put Judeo-Christian principles into practice to build healthy spirits, minds, and bodies for all. We provide young people with the skills and experiences to become healthy, caring, and productive adults and to provide programs that strengthen the family. Our Vision is to be a leader in providing transformational program experiences that will increase each individual's capacity to be a contributing member of society.

For information about both camps, visit www.hayowentha.org and follow camp activities on Facebook at www.facebook.com/hayowenthacamps.

TORCH LAKE SUMMERS

GROWING UP AT CAMP HAYO-WENT HA

by CRAIG HUPP
as told by DAVE KEENA
illustrated by ROB WILKINSON

PREFACE

I spent nine summers as a camper and counselor at Camp Hayo-Went-Ha on Torch Lake. They were among the best times of my life. I am grateful my daughter married into a Torch Lake family. That prompted a renewed acquaintance with a place I dearly loved.

Memory is a funny thing. Some events, unforgettable at the time, disappear completely from memory, replaced by imagined events complete in every detail. Recounting this story almost 50 years later, I am certain of the absolute truth of only a few of the facts recounted herein. One is that Torch Lake is the third most beautiful lake in the world, just as the sign in the Village of Alden proclaims. As for the rest, I cannot be sure now what is true and what is the creation of memory. Perhaps the best course is to regard this memoir as a work of fiction grown, like pearls, around grains of truth.

I almost waited too long to share this story with my children. But a terminal illness is a good motivator. When I was diagnosed with advanced cancer this spring, I decided to take care of unfinished business.

Over the past two months, I have been bedridden and various family members have looked after my care. Somewhat to my surprise, one afternoon my son-in-law Craig Hupp asked me about my time at Torch Lake. Craig's mother Kay passed away a few years ago. Craig told me he regretted he had not asked her about the time before paved roads, electricity, and running water came to the Hupp family cottage on Torch Lake.

I began attending Camp Hayo-Went-Ha in 1934; the same year, I think, his grandparents began summering on Torch Lake in a cottage a mile and a half down the shore from the camp. I have been a regular visitor at the Hupp cottage in the last 15 years, visits that have brought many memories back. The camp's Boat House is visible from the Hupp's cottage and on quiet evenings I can hear

"Taps" floating down on the breeze. I now appreciate how the coincidental Torch Lake connection between the Hupp and Keena families is important to both of us.

Craig was as interested in hearing about the "early" years at Torch as I was interested in telling about them. So, on occasional afternoons this spring, I talked through my years at Hayo-Went-Ha and he took notes. Time will tell what he makes of the story.

Dave Keena, June 1987

After Dave's funeral, I put my notes from conversations with Dave in a box with the thought I would get to them soon. The box sat in my home office on Pemberton, then migrated to the Pemberton attic, and from there to the attic on Notre Dame. Finally, 30 years later, I have the time, found the box in the attic, reread my notes, and put Dave's story in order. I have had the time to research Hayo-Went-Ha in the 1930s and get Dave's high school records from the Fountain Valley School of Colorado. They have permitted me to round out his story. I hope I have done it justice.

Craig Hupp, May 2018

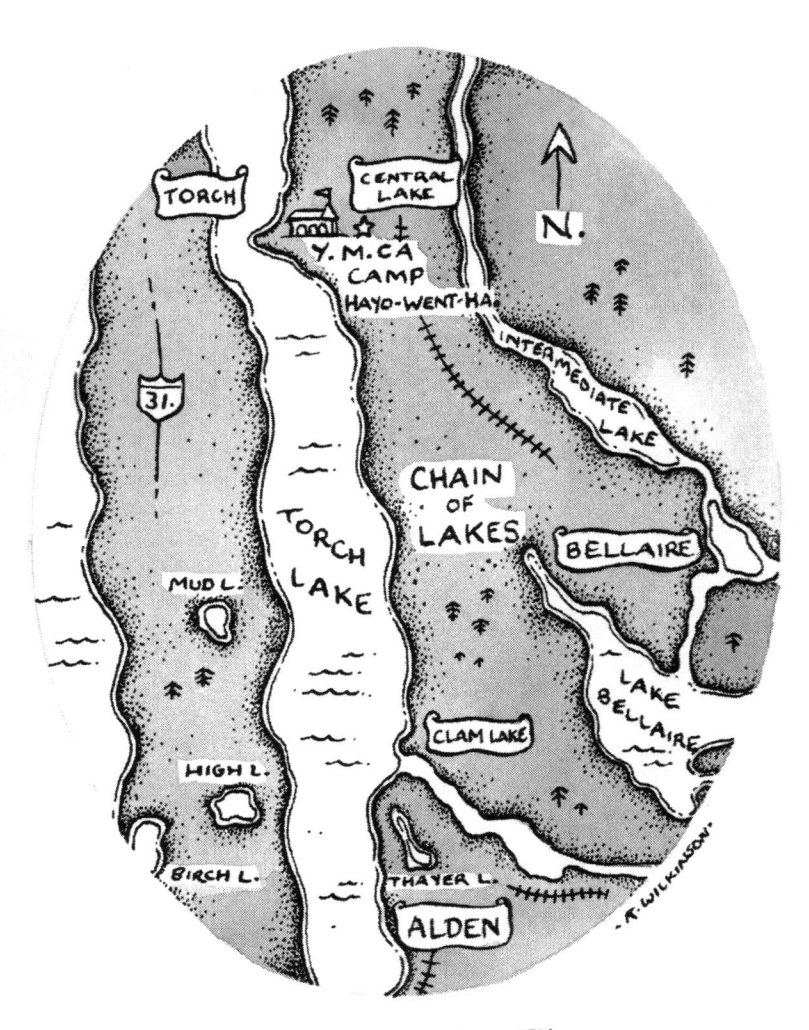

ANTRIM COUNTY.

Dave Keena and Mother, 1926[A]

CHAPTER ONE
I Never Had a Father

My father, James Trafton Keena, was 73 in January 1924 when he died, a successful lawyer and banker in Detroit. Although he was a Democrat (being a staunch Catholic), his clients and social circle were the prominent men in the city, Republicans all. At age 66 he was elected president and later chairman of the board of the Peoples State Bank, the largest bank in Detroit in the early 1920s. He was a humorous after-dinner speaker, sought after for civic and business functions.

I was born on July 5, 1924, into a grieving but well-to-do family at 580 Seyburn Road in Detroit's Indian Village neighborhood, a mile east of downtown Detroit and just two blocks from the amusement palaces and park at the foot of the Belle Isle Bridge. My father left this world five months before I arrived, survived by his second wife Mabel, four young children aged 8 to 14, Margaret (Margie), Paul, and Aileen and Kathleen (twins), and me in utero.

When the patriarch died, his first family were adults; the youngest, Mylne, was 39. The family tale was that my mother, a secretary at my father's law firm, had been engaged to Mylne but had instead married my father, then a widower, in 1909. That was history and not subject to much discussion in my father's second family during my childhood. Mylne lived with my father and my mother until he married in 1922. He remained friends with my mother throughout his life.

My other half-brothers departed Detroit a few years after their mother died, Leo to the consular service and Trafton to open a car dealership in Seattle. Neither were present in my childhood except for short visits (I remember none). My oldest half sibling Pauletta lived in New York. Her first grandchild was born the same year I was!

The male figures in my early youth, such as they were, were my older brother Paul and Arnold, our chauffeur. Paul, eleven years older than I, was a benign presence. I remember being taken by him to Belle Isle and canoeing on the canals. I had to be content with his stories of the roller coaster and other rides at the Electric Park which closed when I was four although I have clear memories of the electric lights at the entrance of the amusement park and the sound of the calliope. Aileen and Kathleen were fourteen years my senior. They attended Sarah Lawrence College in New York. Though they doted on me when home (Aileen in particular — I was Pooh and she was Piglet), their heads were in the debutante world by the time I was six. Margie, next to me in age, was eight years older. She was too much separated in age to be a close friend or pal when I was a child.

So, let me tell you the little I knew or now remember about Arnold, in truth more of a companion than any of my siblings. He was Irish, I think, a Murphy or a Walsh. His duties beyond driving my mother or sisters in the family Packard were minimal. He had time to keep a little boy company. He accompanied my family when we moved from Seyburn to a new home at 460 Lakeland in Grosse Pointe around 1928 and lived in the servants' quarters on the third floor.

Arnold had a knack for whittling simple toys accompanied by complicated tales. We would sit together on the stoop by the back door. I remember watching a top he had carved spin and

I NEVER HAD A FATHER

spin and spin in the driveway. The top had bright yellow and green bands with a red star painted on its top. He told me a genie inside the top kept it balanced while it whirled.

Arnold and I struck up our friendship during Prohibition. He operated some kind of distillery apparatus in the far end of the third floor attic, a foreign country to my mother. I vividly remember the warm Saturday afternoon in November 1931 when there was a muffled explosion upstairs, then smoke, then a general household panic, and finally a frantic call to the Grosse Pointe fire department, just a block away. From my seven-year-old's perspective, the afternoon became even more interesting when a bright red fire engine and nine firemen arrived, siren wailing. I had been an occasional visitor to the firehouse. As a consequence, as my mother and I looked on from the other side of the street, I felt qualified to explain to her how the firemen would put the fire out. Part of the third floor and second floor were damaged but, because the house was so large, we remained in residence during most of the repairs. Arnold left the day after the fire. Only much later did I learn his still caused the explosion.

I was five in October 1929 when the stock market crashed. While I am sure the crash affected my family's financial fortunes, it was far from devastating, at least initially. My twin sisters were "brought out" in 1930 and important family affairs like engagements, weddings and children made the *Detroit Free Press* Society page. The Keena family remained in the *Social Secretary of Detroit* and my mother maintained her many society connections. My brother Paul continued his schooling at Rumford School in Connecticut and Margie continued at the Mary C. Wheeler School in Providence, Rhode Island.

By 1933, our financial circumstances changed, associated with the string of bank failures in Detroit in 1931 and 1932. My mother, who had both foresight and initiative, decided it was time to move to a less expensive house. By 1934, we were established four blocks away at 424 Lincoln, two houses east of St. Paul. That is the house

I grew up in. The large mansions and estates of the automobile elite dominated our neighborhood. Their large side lawns are now occupied by two or three large new houses.

When I finished grade school in 1938, my mother was employed as manager of Goldsbary Flowers on the second floor of the Book Tower on Washington Boulevard in downtown Detroit.

My formal schooling followed the family tradition of private education. It began at age six at Grosse Pointe Country Day on Fisher Road, just a few blocks from home. My older half-brothers Leo, Trafton, and Mylne attended high school at Detroit University School where Leo and Trafton had been star athletes. The school moved from Detroit to Cook Road in Grosse Pointe Farms in 1928 and became the Grosse Pointe University School (known as "GUPAS" to Grosse Pointers). I attended GUPAS for my freshman year in high school. My private school education was made possible only through scholarship and support from "Uncle" Jere Hutchins. Poor grades and straitened finances sent me to Grosse Pointe High School for tenth grade. The high school was next door to Grosse Pointe Country Day. For my junior year, my mother enrolled me in the Fountain Valley School of Colorado in Colorado Springs. My father had loved equestrian sports and Fountain Valley's equestrian programs captured my mother's fancy. More on Fountain Valley later. However, I finished my last semester of formal high school back at Grosse Pointe High.

My real education took place elsewhere. That is the subject of this memoir.

I NEVER HAD A FATHER

Lakeland House[A]

Grosse Pointe Country Day[ULS]

Grosse Pointe High School[GPS]

CHAPTER TWO

First Time to Camp

My home in the 1930s, if home is where the heart is, was on the shores of Torch Lake in northwest Michigan at Camp Hayo-Went-Ha. It was a well-established YMCA summer camp. In June 1934 I received a short, matter-of-fact explanation from my mother of her summer plans for me two weeks before I was dispatched to the big Michigan Central Railway station in downtown Detroit to meet a group of campers headed for Hayo-Went-Ha.

I remember the bustle at home while a maid packed my clothes into a wooden trunk. The camp sent a letter outlining what a camper should bring to camp. It explained that because the camp was "not a fashionable dress resort" (an understatement!), campers should not bring straw hats, derbies or "biled" shirts (starched white shirts boiled to regain their whiteness). Required clothing included "two dark, heavy, double woolen blankets, tennis shoes, extra underclothing and a suit of heavy underclothing, trousers, stockings, outing shirts, extra coat, old cap, woolen sweater, small pillow case filled with hay, soap in a metal box, brush and comb, toothbrush, swimming suit, handkerchiefs and

Bible." Reading between the lines, the message was: Northern Michigan can be cold in the summer. The letter went on to advise a "camera, tennis racquet, fishing tackle, note book and pencil, any good books for boys, mirror, clothes brush, needle and thread, will add to the enjoyment and convenience." Mothers were instructed to pack the clothing and personal effects in a wooden box, no bigger that 30 inches long, 18 inches wide and 15 inches deep, fitted with hinges and a padlock. I remember my mother sewing labels with my name into each article of clothing, something she repeated when each of my children when off to camp many years later.

The polio scares in the early 1930s prompted my mother's decision to send me to camp. Several Grosse Pointe families had sent children to various camps the prior summer hoping to avoid the epidemic.

My mother learned about Hayo-Went-Ha from Ann Vail, the visiting nurse in Grosse Pointe who worked at the camp during the summer. Through Miss Vail my mother met camp director Cliff "Cap" Drury and his wife Edna in the fall of 1933. On their way to and from camp each year the Drurys stayed with friends in Detroit, a month in the spring to complete summer plans, organize supplies, etc. and in late August to tie up the summer's finances. When they met, my mother took an instant liking to the Drurys (everyone did) and was impressed by the camp life they described. Cap was a handsome, athletic, charismatic man of 35. Edna was independent and resourceful, qualities my mother had in spades.

My mother decided then and there and committed me for the summer of 1934, but did not share her plan with me until the end of the school year the following spring.

I am sure that my mother's involvement in the YWCA influenced her decision to send me to a camp run by the YMCA. She had attended the national YWCA convention in Minneapolis in 1932.

My escort to the train was "Uncle" Jere Hutchins, a long-time business associate of my father's. Mr. Hutchins, who was childless, played the role of favorite "uncle" when I was growing up. Uncle Jere had come to Detroit in 1894 to

FIRST TIME TO CAMP

manage one of the streetcar companies. Over the next two decades he merged the local street car companies into the Detroit United Railways Company and added interurban companies with a network of lines in southeast Michigan. He ran the DUR until 1922 when the city of Detroit forced a takeover of the street railways system. His energy was undiminished, and I received the benefit of attention he had devoted to the DUR.

In his retirement, Uncle Jere had moved to his farm on Cook Road in what is now Grosse Pointe Farms. He had given part of his farm to Detroit University School to help its move to Grosse Pointe. The 30-minute walk from our house on Lincoln to his farmhouse, cutting across the Country Club of Detroit golf course, was always worth the welcome I received on my arrival.

Uncle Jere was quite a sport. He told exciting tales of his adventures out west before he moved to Detroit. He had grown up on a plantation in Louisiana. As a young man, he became a cowboy in Texas, then an editor of the *Waco Examiner* riding the county to gather stories, and later an engineer building railroads in Kansas. Uncle Jere told great stories about camping in the out-of-doors. He had been one of the first Grosse Pointers to take to the air, flying with Frank Coffyn on an aerial tour of Lake St. Clair in June 1911. I kept a framed photo of Uncle Jere in the Wright biplane on my bedroom dresser for many years.

On Saturday, June 23, 1934, Uncle Jere treated me to an early dinner at a restaurant on Michigan Avenue, a block from Briggs Stadium and two blocks from the train station. That was a regular stop on Saturdays when Uncle Jere took me to Tiger baseball games, his favorite pastime. The Tigers were away that Saturday but whenever the Tigers' schedule coincided with my trip to Hayo-Went-Ha, we coupled lunch with a Tigers game (always at 1:06 p.m. — Briggs Stadium did not get lights until after the war) because my train did not leave until around 5 p.m.

In 1934 over dinner before boarding the train, he retold stories of his nights under the stars. He expressed both envy

9

TORCH LAKE SUMMERS

LOG CABIN SIX.

FIRST TIME TO CAMP

and pleasure I would have a summer filled with camping. He wanted to know whether the camp offered horseback riding. "Nothing is better than inspecting the world from the back of a horse." I told him I did not know but promised to try horseback riding if it was offered.

I am sure he told me to behave myself on the trip, but any such warning was perfunctory because Uncle Jere remained a boy at heart, although he was over 80 in 1934.

Uncle Jere made sure I had a packet of two sandwiches, fruit and a large slice of chocolate cake specially wrapped by the restaurant kitchen to hold me over until I reached camp. He oversaw the porter who handled my trunk and accompanied me onto the sleeping car where at least a dozen other Hayo-Went-Ha campers were assembled. He turned me over to the care of Bill Dewey, a counselor on his way to camp. Uncle Jere wished me well, told me to write my mother weekly, and said he looked forward to letters from me. Then we shook hands solemnly and my life at Hayo-Went-Ha began.

As the youngest in a household of society women, I had become a self-sufficient male and was confident in my little world. I had seen some of the larger world on streetcar rides around the east side of Detroit. While I would be wrong to claim I felt no trepidation about this trip to northern Michigan, I was excited by the adventure of a summer at camp, encouraged by Uncle Jere's stories and those of the returning campers I met on the train.

We left Detroit at 5 p.m. for the overnight trip north. Bill Dewey, a five-year camp veteran, had no difficulty in keeping eleven campers aged 9 to 14 corralled, but I remember him spoiling none of the fun we had on my first overnight trip to Central Lake.

Most of the train trip was passed in darkness. It became boring over the years. The first trip was interesting because it was the first. After the first year, my eagerness to reach camp and renew friendships offset the tedium of the overnight journey north. The return trip in August was different; the prospect of summer's end and another school year magnified the discomfort of the overnight return trip.

Ben Harmon, another 10-year-old, and I saw too little out the window to keep us occupied. We explored the train, all four passenger cars, and stood on the rear platform on the last car, watching the trees flash by and then recede in the distance. We returned covered with ash and cinders from the locomotive. The scrubbing we got from Bill Dewey was just a little heartier than needed, to discourage similar adventures on the rest of the trip.

Later trips to camp were devoted to renewing friendships, telling lies about sports and girls, and playing cards. The YMCA did not permit gambling, so we never strayed into poker. Later, the army schooled me in that game, mostly at my expense. Other campers introduced me first to gin rummy. In time, we moved on to pinochle and then bridge. For the last three summers, Ben Harmon, Tommy Baldwin, Jerry Greenwood and I (by then all camp counselors) had a regular foursome to begin and end the summer.

Only one trip north over the years, other than my first, was particularly memorable. In 1936 or '37, a derailment north of Grand Rapids delayed our train north for several hours. I remember getting out and examining the overturned engine and cars. No one had been seriously injured as I recall now, but afterwards I embellished my story of the wreck with dead and injured passengers strewn across the tracks. Ben had a Brownie camera and took my picture in front of the locomotive's driving wheels. I kept the photo on my desk at Fountain Valley, a visual aid to my story of the train wreck.

We rode the Michigan Central northwest to Grand Rapids and changed to a Pere Marquette train to reach Traverse City. The Hayo-Went-Ha party grew in Lansing and again in Grand Rapids when boys from the middle of the state and Chicago joined us and another contingent boarded in Traverse City. The train stopped to pick up an occasional camper in the little towns we passed along the way. By the time we arrived in Traverse City we had commandeered two entire cars and sometimes overflowed into a third. From

FIRST TIME TO CAMP

Grand Rapids to Traverse City there was not much to see as we passed through scrub regrowth from areas that had been clear-cut 30 years earlier. We crossed the long trestle over the Manistee gorge in darkness. I passed under that bridge three times on canoe trips down the Manistee and marveled how high the spans were above our heads.

At Traverse City we usually had time to get breakfast near the station. We changed trains to the Pere Marquette line that meandered around the chain of lakes from Traverse City to Petoskey, passing through Acme, Bates, Williamsburg, Mable, Barker Creek, Rapid City, Alden, Comfort, Bellaire, and Snow Flake to reach, at long last, Central Lake. We filled the local train to Central Lake, making it the Hayo-Went-Ha special. Between Traverse City and Central Lake, principal stops were the villages of Alden and Bellaire, while most of the other "stops" on the published schedule were just flag crossings where passengers, if any, waved the train down. We could smell the north woods. The early morning air was still crisp in late June, hinting at what we could expect for the first week in our cabins at camp. We opened the passenger car windows, despite objections from the more tender campers. Often we could see our breath in the cold morning air. The day always warmed as we traveled to Central Lake.

Our appetites for camp were whetted on the Pere Marquette. When we left Traverse City, we traveled for several miles along Grand Traverse East Bay and then, crossing hills to the east, left glimpses of the Bay behind us as we caught sight of Elk and Round Lakes. As we approached Alden, the tracks ran along the east shore of Torch Lake. Often the train made a leisurely stop in Alden, giving the more daring campers time to dash for a quick wade in Torch Lake. One year, two boys from Chicago did not get back to the station in time and spent the day in Alden until a staff member arrived in the evening to fetch them. Approaching Bellaire, we had glimpses of Lake Bellaire to tantalize us. We knew we were in the home stretch leaving Bellaire because the tracks ran along Intermediate Lake.

The last stop before Central Lake was the the Snow Flake Spiritualist Camp. As the stop approached, counselors told the youngest campers stories of spiritualists who communicated with those who had passed beyond. Everyone "knew" to stay away from the spiritualist camp during Thursday night camp meetings when the spiritualists practiced dark arts. Infrequently, the train picked up or discharged passengers at Snow Flake. They became the objects of much curiosity for the Hayo-Went-Ha boys. On the hike from Central Lake to Hayo-Went-Ha, we speculated about these mysterious travelers, many of whom were thought to have a sinister look.

As soon as we saw Intermediate Lake, camp counselors led us in camp songs for the last 20 minutes of our train journey, always beginning with the "Camp Song" written in 1936 by Hugh Vail:

Camp days dear Old Torch is blue,
We recall them all.
On the sloping pine hills, in the dining hall.
Ne'er will we forget thee
Nor our founders three,
Back at Hayo-Went-Ha,
Each for all are we.
So come all be loyal to your choo-choo-hurrah
Choo-choo-hurah,
Choo-choo-hurah-rah-rah-rah,
Come all be loyal with your choo-choo-hurrah
Choo-choo-hurah for Hayo-Went-Ha
Rah, Rah, Rah, Rah, Rah.

It was a merry crew that spilled out of the train at the conductor's whistle when the train coasted to a stop in Central Lake.

Central Lake is little changed from the village in the 1930s. Then as now it was a sleepy village of 600 souls, nestled against a line of hills separating Intermediate and Torch Lakes. It was a perennial topic of discussion why the lake was called Intermediate but the village called Central. A camp truck

FIRST TIME TO CAMP

driven by Clarence "Handy" Hansen met us at the depot and we hoisted our trunks on board. We had an hour to visit Bachmann's Five & Dime for any last-minute purchases or necessaries. Those were loaded on the truck. Then, with a grinding of gears, it disappeared up the hill and we set off on foot for camp.

During our first hike of the year, the treatment of the girls arriving for the girls camp, Four-Way Lodge, would come up. Four-Way was a mile south of Hayo-Went-Ha. They arrived by train at Central Lake as we did. Villagers turned out for the girls' arrival and a pool of cars and trucks transported the girls to camp, sparing them the hike. The younger boys grumbled about the injustice of such unequal treatment and the weakness of womanhood, while the oldest boys and counselors kept their thoughts on the fantasy of an expedition to the Four-Way Lodge after hours.

The first mile west out of the village is a steady grade up Dean's Hill. Campers with new boots began to complain before we reached the crest. I thought my feet would fall off and was sure I was hiking to a camp in the mountains. But we new campers soon learned what the camp was all about. The counselors and older boys set an example of good cheer and encouragement. When the youngest, the ten-year-olds, tuckered out, older boys hoisted them up on their backs and carried them for a while. That is when I heard "Each for all and all for each" the first time.

Dennis Applewood was a camper three years ahead of me. His father was the doctor in Central Lake. He is one of the few townies I recall as a camper. He told us how in the winter under the right conditions, you could sled from the top of Dean's Hill through town and across the bridge over Intermediate Lake. To enjoy the thrill of a mile-long sled or toboggan ride, most of us would have trudged up the hill in the cold. On a warm June day, I could not imagine how cold my feet would be when I reached the top of the hill and turned around to sled down. Even today a long sled ride down that hill seems worth the cold march to the top.

Every year we began the same song as we passed the last house in the village. The farm at the top was the Walbrecht Farm. I don't remember the song's title but the lines I remember go:

Little town at the bottom,
Walbrecht's barn at the top.
Up the hill to Torch Lake
We shall not stop.

With the chorus:

It's 'Up Dean Hill,' and 'Off we go.'
Hayo-Went-Ha's not too far to go.
Step quick and step fast,
We'll make the miles fly past.

Other verses included:

Keep strong lads, keep strong.
We know our march is long.
Torch Lake is over the hill.
There you all can drink your fill.

Now stride 'round Springstead's Corner
And trot down that wooded lane.
Our long hike is nearly over.
We're back at camp again.

There were more verses and many other songs to inspire our tired legs. It was a tough hike because we had not been hardened up by the camp activities ahead of us.

When we rounded the top of the hill and saw the Walbrecht's red barn on the left, we knew the worst was over. We had a two-mile gentle downgrade to reach Torch Lake and then turned left for the last mile to the camp.

Antrim County was lumbered at the turn of the century. The tall trees of today were little more than scrub growth in

FIRST TIME TO CAMP

the mid 1930s. From the top of Dean's Hill and at several points on the down grade you could see the blue water of Torch Lake. We often raced ahead to claim the first view.

If you took a short detour up the ridge line to Walbrecht's barn, you could see as far as the East Bay of Grand Traverse Bay. One summer on a hike to Central Lake we stopped by the Walbrechts and asked if we could climb the ladder up the outside the barn's silo. Mr. Walbrecht agreed. Not every hiker was brave enough to climb 45 feet up the ladder. It took every ounce of my courage to get on that ladder because I hated heights. But I was the second oldest in the hiking party and too proud to be shown up in front of younger campers.

The view was worth the climb. I could see forever, looking over Torch and both East and West Bays of Grand Traverse Bay. Past the south end of Torch Lake, there was a glimmer of blue from Elk Lake. I could glimpse the camp's Boat House through the trees and see white sails out on Torch. The breeze was stronger at the top of the silo and whooshed around the rungs of the ladder and over the silo's cupola. Going down the ladder was even worse than going up. I held on with a death grip to the rung above me as I felt around with my foot, struggling to find the rung below. It seemed to take forever to reach the bottom and step off the ladder onto firm ground.

Springstead's Corner in the song was the junction of the Central Lake and Torch Lake roads, named by the campers for an old mailbox on a farm lane near the junction. At a road end to the lake, we always stopped to drink, fill canteens and splash water on our faces. However, swimming had to wait until we reached camp.

In 1934, the last mile to camp was a walk in the woods. The road along the lake was little more than a two-track, narrow and sandy, and just wide enough for a farm cart or automobile. The road jogged left and right to avoid the largest trees. It passed between wooded and open areas. If it had rained the day before, we were assured of a muddy hike.

By the mid 1930s, the camp had activities on both sides of this two-track road. Concerned about the hazard of the occasional car passing through the camp at high speed (30 miles per hour at most), Cap arranged with the county road commission to move the Torch Lake road to its present location east of the camp, leaving the former county road as a lane that still passes through camp. In exchange, the camp received the land between the old road and the new one. As part of the arrangement, Cap put the older campers to work helping create the new right-of-way. I was grateful twelve-year-olds were not dragooned into the labor detail.

The east shore of Torch had few seasonal or permanent houses. There were only three driveways between Springstead's Corner and the camp entrance. During the whole hike, we might see one or two cars at most and an occasional tractor on the few farm fields between Central Lake and Springstead's Corner.

One year a short rainstorm caught us just after we had passed the crest of Dean's Hill. The afternoon had been gray, and a line of dark clouds appeared over Torch Lake. We picked up our pace hoping to reach camp before the rain started but, after a few warning sprinkles, it began to rain in earnest. After a mad dash for a line of trees 100 yards ahead, we huddled under the trees for ten minutes until the brief storm passed. I don't remember being too wet. The sun appeared, and we dried out by the time we reached the Springstead's Corner.

In later years, the rain storm, as described to new campers as we crested Dean's Hill, became a deluge with thunder and lightning. My memorable addition to the tale, taking advantage of a large dead maple in a field on the north side of the road, was that, in the middle of the storm, lightning struck the tree next to us, setting it on fire. I pointed to the dead maple as proof. Thus are camp legends made.

Our arrival at camp was not complete until we found our trunks, reached our cabins, and put our things away. By this time, it was 6:30 p.m. but sunset was still three hours away.

The camp ran on a regular schedule. But on the day of our arrival, the usual schedule of dinner at 6 p.m. was dispensed with and, after a short orientation talk from Charlie Booth, one of the two counselors assigned to our cabin (Cabin 6), a bugle call announced our first Torch Lake swim session. There was no effort to keep order on the mad dash to the water. Counselors warned the new campers that ice might still be floating in the lake, a story I did not believe until I hit the water the first time. I am sure our screams were heard across the lake, or at least would have been if there had been a house in sight on the far shore. The day ended with a bonfire at the beach where Cap and the counselors told stories that introduced us to the camp's great traditions.

As the stories ended, "Taps" sounded, a musical signature I heard every evening at camp and many evenings in my years in the army. Some nights Karl Sherwood, the bugler during my first years at the camp, played his bugle from a canoe on the lake. On shore, we recited the words.

Day is done, gone the sun,
From the lake, from the hills, from the sky;
All is well, safely rest, God is nigh.

On quiet summer evenings in the early 1970s on my son-in-law's dock a mile down the shore from the camp, the camp bugler's notes took me back to the good times at camp and to the hardest times I experienced in the war.

Thanks and praise, for our days,
'Neath the sun, 'neath the stars, neath the sky;
As we go, this we know, God is nigh.

I had none of that history when I listened to "Taps" for the first time. The bugle call reminded me of a cavalry charge, echoing the romance of Uncle Jere's cowboy tales.

After a night and day on the train, a five-mile hike to camp, a swim in Torch, a hearty meal, and a ceremony around the bonfire, I was asleep on my feet before I reached the top of the steps from the beach. Charlie Booth herded us ten new campers into Cabin 6 in the dark. I have never slept so well.

Uncle Jere Hutchins[JCH]

Uncle Jere in Airplane[DPL]

FIRST TIME TO CAMP

Pere Marquette Wreck[MSU]

Alden Depot[MSU]

TORCH LAKE SUMMERS

Central Lake Depot[HWH]

Old Torch Lake Road[PG]

FIRST TIME TO CAMP

Hayo-Went-Ha Sign[HWH]

Camp Entrance[HWH]

TORCH LAKE SUMMERS

Dave Keena, 1934 (Center)[HWH]

CHAPTER THREE

Million Dollar Mornings

My nine years of camp life began at 6:30 a.m. Monday, June 26, 1934, when a bugle sang out "Reveille," fracturing the early morning silence, followed by the shout, "Everybody up! It's a million-dollar morning." The sunrise prophet was Cap Drury, our camp director. He led by example each morning as he did in everything involving the camp. In 1943 on a troop ship to England, I calculated I spent ("received" is perhaps the better word) 546 million-dollar mornings at Hayo-Went-Ha. My first day at camp in 1934 and my last day in August 1942 and almost every day in between started with that call and then a dash to the lake.

The shock of Torch Lake's icy water in June would wake anyone dead for less than a week, but no one died from the shock. Cap's enthusiasm, ingrained in all campers by the 3rd or 4th morning, had a warming effect. You can be sure we all reached breakfast at 7 a.m. with an appetite.

In telling my story of summers on Torch Lake, perhaps the hardest part is preventing it from becoming a paean to Cap. Not that he does not deserve one, just I cannot do him justice. If I gave him the space in this story commensurate with the impact he had on me during my summers, he would take my story over. So, let me describe him briefly now; then carry his presence with you as you read the story that follows.

Cap became a father figure and role model for me — something I am sure is true for most campers from his era. He had a clear vision of character and development of values. He lived that vision and taught, no, showed us how to achieve it.

I first encountered Cap's leadership approach on my third morning at camp when I entered the bathroom building 45 minutes before "Reveille." I was surprised to find anyone else there, then very surprised to discover it was the camp director cleaning the bathroom. I was not the first junior camper to be so surprised, but he explained he did it every day.

"Dave, we grow by taking on the hard tasks. We lead by showing others how the hard work is the most important to accomplish, but it is never so hard in the doing as in the thinking of it. Besides, Torch Lake is so cold some mornings that unless I have already worked up a sweat, I swear, that water nearly kills me."

He tossed me a mop, and said, "Tell me what a boy gets up to in Grosse Pointe." Helping him finish the bathroom while he drew out details of my life in Grosse Pointe and my thoughts after two days in camp, I learned the lesson he intended; but when I jumped in the lake 45 minutes later, I decided his line about hard work making the lake seem warmer was just a bunch of bull. It sure didn't work for me.

Cap's theme was reflected in a Negro spiritual, one of his favorite songs around a campfire.

> Oh, you gotta have a Glory,
> In the thing you do,
> A Halleluiah Chorus.
> In the Heart of you,
> Paint, or tell a story,
> Sing or shovel coal,
> But, you gotta have a Glory,
> Or the job lacks soul.

Cap knit summers together. His personality drew in like-minded staff and counselors. Cap had an immense sense of fun and boundless energy; every activity he joined in became livelier, more intense. He gave you his undivided attention, perhaps the greatest gift any growing boy can receive. Cap was an excellent judge of the good character often camouflaged in adolescent misbehavior. He offered responsibility and opportunity when boys were prepared to grow. And, most important, Cap was a reliable source of counsel on things great and small. He had a way of seeing the "right" way or "right" solution and helping young men reach the same point with simple words and logic.

I must also introduce Clarence "Handy" Hansen who met us at the train in the last chapter. Clarence had a hand in everything at the camp. Before summer ended, every camper had assisted Clarence on one or more of his projects around the camp. Like Cap, he gave responsibility freely and had an exquisite sense of how much each boy could handle. He had the best stories about camp history, most of which ended in laughter.

Now, on to camp life.

I had the less than noteworthy distinction of being not only the youngest but also the smallest camper in 1934. The youngest campers were 10-year-olds, but I did not turn 10 until two weeks after I arrived in camp. There were occasional exceptions, I being one. For all I know, my mother, intent on sending me away to camp, told the Cap I would turn 10 in early June, instead of July. My real age did not emerge until I had been a camp a few days, and by then I was ensconced in Cabin 6 and my 10th birthday had passed.

I took to camp. My world at home was dominated by family members, all adults or nearly so. Besides my mother and three older sisters, for a time in the mid 1930s my older brother Paul and his wife Suzanne moved back to 424 Lincoln. There were far too many parents/adults/siblings supervising one 10-year-old boy!

I relished the large circle of boys and the many activities

CLIFF 'CAP' DRURY.

available at camp. There never was a lack of things to do or someone to do them with. In spite of my small size, I did not suffer from much teasing and the little I received was good natured.

I liked the water activities best, which was just as well because most days started with a swim in Torch. Thank heavens the lake warmed up in early July. The prevailing wind is from the north and the camp sits on a point with the swimming area in the cove on the south side of the point. Although I had no experience swimming when the summer began, I could swim as well as many of the 12-year-olds by summer's end. Bill Dewey, who taught swimming, attributed my progress to the fact I was too light to sink. That could have been true. I also loved sailing which was the highlight of my afternoons for the first three years at camp.

The youngest campers started off on a two-day overnight camping trip east of camp. The forest was still recovering from the timbering around the turn of the century. While most trees were less than 25 feet tall, the scrubby underbrush was dense. I found I liked being out in the woods.

Our short trip involved cooking four meals — two dinners and two breakfasts. Each boy helped prepare two meals and clean up two meals. I preferred the former activity and resolved that, whenever possible, I would get on the cooking detail and avoid KP. I had no occasion to cook at home and, for most of my first 10 years, a domestic servant had that duty. I came to enjoy cooking and during my time at camp acquired a reputation as a breakfast chef.

I remember little of that first trip except the fire tower. One aftermath of Michigan's timber industry was monumental forest fires in the timber slash during the decades after lumbering ended. In the 1920s, the Michigan Fire Service erected a tall steel lacework fire tower on the hills east of camp. In periods of drought, the Service posted a watcher on the tower who could see for miles in every direction from his perch. A ritual of a camper's first camping trip was to climb the tower. I am glad I only had to do it once. The view was fabulous but not good enough to induce me to go 50 feet up and down the steel rungs on the outside of the tower leg again.

Each summer, the hardest day was the last. Any homesickness from the first few days at camp was long gone. Camp ended the third week in August when the weather was still good and the lake warm. We saw no reason to leave and few of us were eager to exchange camping, hiking, and sports for school. Counselors stayed on for a week after camp to close the camp up. We campers helped with end-of-summer tasks. I loved the water, and it was hard to help put the boats away that last week.

On the last night, we would gather for a final bonfire on the beach. Cap would lead stories and songs around the campfire as the campers and staff would join in.

The song I remember best from my first camp fire is "Hey, Hey, Hey, Hayo-Went-Ha."

> A campfire dies; another lights again
> Alive with memories that sing in the wind.
> And I know where I'm going 'cause I know
> where I've been.
> And, it's hey, hey, hey, Hayo-Went-Ha
> And it's here I want to be one summer more,
> On Hayo-Went-Ha's hills and trails by the shore,
> Where three brothers walked 30 years before,
> And others will walk 100 years more,
> And I'm here because I know what I'm walking for.
> And it's hey, hey, hey, Hayo-Went-Ha.

Each cabin would select a spokesman to sum up the highlights of the cabin's summer. I don't remember who spoke for Cabin 6; I was too shy to be the spokesman.

As the ceremony ended campers, staff, and leaders formed a large circle around the fire. Candles were handed around each side until everyone had one. Then Cap would lean in to the campfire to light his candle. He would gaze around the circle at the faces dimly lit by the campfire's light. He told us we had learned much that summer, from the teachings of Chief Hayo-Went-Ha, from the spirits of the woods and the lake, and from fellow campers. He reminded us of the Indian Fire Ceremony and asked us to recall the wisdom shared around that campfire.

Cap closed by asking us to promise that in the year ahead we would live the lessons and wisdom of Hayo-Went-Ha. He then turned and lit the candles of the campers on his left and right, saying, "Seal your promise with the pledge to 'Keep the Flame Burning.'" The campers turned to the person next to them, lighting their candle and repeating the pledge to "Keep the Flame Burning." Slowly the light spread around the circle to a steady murmur of "Keep the Flame Burning." When the 140 candles were lit, Cap finished, "Remember, because your candle will dim and go out, you must keep the flame burning in your heart until we meet again." At that we extinguished our candles and, in a quiet mood, found our sleeping bags, lay down on the beach and fell asleep under the stars for the last time that summer.

Gradually we would drop off to sleep until all was quiet. We had the stars, planets, and meteors overhead, the sound of the waves lapping on the beach and the caress of a gentle night breeze on the lake to lull us to sleep. For much of the 1930s, a pair of barred owls nested in the northern area of the camp and we often listened to their calls, "Who:who — who:whooo," at twilight. One memorable night, their calls kept us company for at least an hour as the moon rose on the eastern shore. Another year, the closing ceremony coincided with the Perseid meteor shower and we watched shooting stars until sleep carried us away. Both made a great send off and became part of camp lore.

On the day of our departure, always a Saturday, we spent a great deal of time packing — which meant scouring camp for clothing and equipment mislaid over the summer, its absence sure to be noticed and commented on when we unpacked at home. At 4 p.m., we had an early dinner and then the Central Lake shuttle began. At summer's end, we were spared the hike to town. It took five round trips on the camp's trucks to get us all into Central Lake with our gear. Each cabin departed together shepherded by its counselors, the older cabins first.

Central Lake had a village fair on the third weekend in August. It provided us with amusement until our counselors rounded us up for the evening train. We spent what pocket money we had left at the drugstore or at Bachmann's.

The southbound Pere Marquette train arrived at 10 p.m. and with a certain amount of confusion, we boarded sleeping cars, segregated by destination, Detroit or Chicago. The Detroit boys filled two cars. Later, in the years when I was a counselor and responsible for a cabin, I remember spending a hectic hour before the train arrived, rounding up my cabin mates and helping other counselors find their missing campers. Fortunately, there was a one-hour layover in Traverse City where our sleeping cars were coupled to through trains to Detroit or Chicago, so the local train could be held a few minutes without disrupting the train schedule. On several occasions, there was a fair amount of begging and pleading with the railroad engineer to hold the train for another minute or two as the last camper was found. I don't recall leaving any boy behind, but there was always another train the next day. The trip home passed in darkness until around Lansing. I arrived in Detroit after my first summer at Torch in the late morning of Sunday, August 19.

Uncle Jere was at the Michigan Central station to greet me, a tradition that continued until 1939. We stopped at the Detroit Athletic Club for lunch. In later years if the Detroit Tigers were in town, we lunched on hot dogs in Uncle Jere's box seats behind third base and watched the baseball game.

That first year, I talked nonstop during lunch about life at camp. Uncle Jere was hard of hearing. I think he learned more about my wonderful summer from my enthusiasm and volubility than from the sentences that boiled past my lips. I was home by 2 p.m. I took at least two nights to get used to a proper bed. My sleep in a bedroom alone was restless; I missed the night time sounds of eleven other sleepers and the northern woods. But, I did not miss the call to reveille and slept until noon.

Cap Drury[HWH]

Morning Swim[HWH]

MILLION DOLLAR MORNINGS

Diving Platform[HWH]

Sailing[HWH]

The Fire Tower[HWH]

CHAPTER FOUR

The Camp and Its Traditions

Let me tell you a little about the camp in the mid to late 1930s.

"The Founders Three" was the origin story for Camp Hayo-Went-Ha. Lincoln Buell, C.W. Wagner, and William Gay, all leaders in the Young Men's Christian Association in their home towns, founded the camp in 1904. They envisioned a summer camp based on Christian values to give boys an outdoor experience and build character.

I never learned what brought the three men to Alden as opposed to another village in northern Michigan. They stepped off the Pere Marquette train at the Alden depot in May 1904, hoisted packs on their backs, and headed north along the east shore of Torch Lake in search of the perfect site for a summer camp. There were just a few dwellings between Alden and Eastport at the north end of the lake — several farmhouses, two one-room schools, a store at the ferry at Clam River, and the occasional driveway meandering towards a primitive cottage by the lake shore. It was a two-day hike, an exploration really, as the men walked north. They occasionally deviated from the two-track to hike to the lake, to peer up and down the shore and then return to the two-track, to walk farther north and repeat the detour.

When the first day ended, they had hiked nearly eight miles north from Alden. They walked down a road end to the lake to camp for the night and saw Tyler's Point six miles north. The point had a commanding view of the length of the lake. It had not been timbered, unlike most of the other land nearby, and the cedar trees glowed green in the setting sun. The Founders Three reached Tyler's Point the next day and recognized it as the place for the camp of their dreams. They camped there for three days, exploring the shore and hills behind the camp.

They were men of action. They resolved to discover who owned it and to make an offer as soon as possible. A six-hour hike took them to Bellaire, the county seat, and discussions with the Register of Deeds who identified a Mr. William Tyler as the owner of the property. Once they agreed Tyler's Point was the location for their summer camp, the Founders Three hiked three hours to Central Lake where Mr. Tyler lived, arriving late in the afternoon.

Mr. Tyler told them he had no interest in selling the property because he intended to preserve the timber on the point. Mr. Tyler's initial rebuff did not discourage the Founders Three. They described at great length their vision for the camp — a place where boys could grow to be men and leaders. They described the founding principles of the YMCA, an organization to develop boys into men founded on Christian principles with prayer and devotional readings every day and service on Sunday. They spoke of the benefits of pure air and clean water for boys living in towns and cities with few opportunities to learn self-reliance and gain confidence in themselves as leaders. They told Mr. Tyler they had felt God's presence manifest in the natural beauty of the point, in the whispers of the breeze in the pines, in the sunset over the western shore, and in songs of the birds at dawn and dusk.

After an hour, the Founders Three convinced Mr. Tyler — and they truly did because he agreed to lease his property for 10 years for only $20. By that time, evening was upon them

THE CAMP AND ITS TRADITIONS

and it was too late to hike back to Tyler's Point. Mr. Tyler invited the Founders Three to dinner with his family and put them up for the night.

The following day, May 28, the Founders Three located an adjoining property owner and purchased his property outright. They spent the rest of the day in Central Lake with an attorney who drafted the legal documents. By the time they hiked over the hill from Central Lake to return to Tyler's Point (the first Hayo-Went-Ha hike from town to camp), they had secured over 50 acres for their camp.

The next afternoon, the Founders Three stood on Tyler's Point — now their point! — and waved down the steamer *Mabel* on her way to Alden from Eastport. At 4 p.m. that afternoon, they waded out to the *Mabel* and began their journey to back Grand Rapids, having accomplished the first step toward their dream of a camp for young men on Torch Lake.

Determined to start the camp that summer, they spent the next two months at a feverish pace, organizing everything needed for a two-week camp outing, and soliciting the first group of campers. They succeeded. On August 2, 15 campers arrived and life at Camp Hayo-Went-Ha began.

The Founders Three's vision for a boys summer camp on Torch was so compelling that before the camp opened in 1905, the business men in Central Lake had raised $350 dollars and purchased another 25 acres for the camp. Over the years the camp acquired more property and shoreline, so that by my arrival in mid 1930s, Hayo-Went-Ha consisted of the hundreds of acres and over a mile of shoreline. There were about 140 campers and counselors each summer and seven staff.

The camp took its name from Hayo-Went-Ha, a mythical Iroquois chief immortalized in Benjamin Hathaway's *The League of the Iroquois*. Hathaway's summary of Hayo-Went-Ha's character captured the spirit the Founders Three sought to promote.

THE AMPHITHEATRE.

THE CAMP AND ITS TRADITIONS

> What knowledge, virtue else hath he,
> In worthy work — deeds nobly done —
> He best may teach men quick to see
> The meaning of a battle won.

When I arrived, there were many permanent structures, most prominent was the Boat House which still overlooks the bathing area today. By tradition, counselors carved their names or initials into the exposed beams in its lower level. I received that honor when I became a junior counselor in 1939. I could barely find my "DPK" when I took my son David to camp in 1970.

When I arrived, the dining hall was a roofed structure with open sides, large enough to serve 100 boys at once. In my third year, it was replaced by what is now the "Old Dining Hall," an enclosed building and a great improvement on cold or rainy days. There were other buildings housing activities, staff administration, and storage. The New Lodge (renamed Bonbright Lodge after I left) was built in 1930. It had a stage, more on that in a later chapter.

We had several places to gather. Most important was the Indian Council Ring used only once or twice a summer. In addition, there was an earthen amphitheater on the beach facing the lake, centered on a fire pit. The open-air Chapel was a semi-circle of benches in the woods by Tyler's Point and our gathering place every Sunday morning for service. The athletic fields had been expanded before 1934 and included tennis courts and graded fields for baseball and other sports on the far side of the old Torch Lake road.

There were 12 cabins, two on the beach by the lake and ten 100 feet back from the lake. The cabins are still there and little changed from 50 years ago. They face the south end of the lake. They have large unscreened windows with solid horizontal shutters on every side. When closed, the shutters provided but a minor barrier to strong winds from the south. Open or closed, they provided no obstacles to insects that came and went at will. Fortunately, there were few. But for the roof, we could have been sleeping out of doors. When it rained, the patter on the roof made my warmth inside my blankets so much more delicious. But, in the darkness of a rainy morning, we dreaded the call of "It's a million dollar morning," and the wet dash to the lake or the dining hall. Waves breaking a few feet away, whether a calm murmur or a low roar in a storm, provided our bedtime lullaby. I have never slept so well.

Each cabin held ten campers and two counselors sleeping on bunk beds. Each camper placed his trunk at the end of his bunk bed. Between the morning swim and breakfast, we made up our beds and policed both inside and around the cabin.

The bathroom building was a few steps away. It had four flush toilets fed by a cistern with water pumped from a camp well. Until electricity reached the camp around 1940, filling the cistern twice a day with a hand pump was a duty shared by all campers. Four boys were assigned to the task, alternating two-minute turns at the pump handle. The cistern held 636 gallons, a volume the boys memorized because each up-and-down of the pump handle produced one-half gallon of water. That meant 1272 pumps were needed. Campers interpreted the slogan "Each for all and all for each" to mean no boy had to pump more than one quarter of the pumps needed to fill the cistern. We quickly learned our share of the work equaled 318 pumps of the handle, no more, no less. At 40 pumps a minute, a pace that grew easier as the summer progressed, we could fill the cistern in half an hour. Everyone shared the task which meant each boy had to help fill the cistern three to four times a summer.

The spring and its stream meandering through the camp had been tamed and an earlier spring box used to keep camp perishables cool had been replaced with a culvert with an opening through which perishables were dangled in the stream.

CAMP ACTIVITIES

The camp schedule followed this general pattern most days, but there were often exceptions.

6:30	Reveille. Dip in the lake. Setting-up exercises
7:00	Breakfast
7:30	Camp Duties - Blankets out for airing, etc.
8:00	Morning inspection
8:15	Bible Study - Announcement of the day's events
9:00	Activities and nature study - Photography - Tennis - Manual training - Hikes - Fishing - Boating, etc.
11:00	Swimming period
12:00	Dinner
12:30	Store and bank open
1:00	Rest hour
2:00	Athletics
4:00	Swimming period
5:30	Evening inspection
6:00	Supper
7:00	Twilight games and amusements
8:00	Camp fire or evening entertainment
9:00	Warning whistle
9:30	"Taps," and lights out

Most weeks, a dozen or more boys would be away on camping or canoeing trips.

A boy would have been dead if he could not find half-a-dozen activities of interest every day. We had a choice of baseball, tennis, football (in August only, to match the college schedule, and my favorite sport), archery and badminton. In 1940 with the war in Europe, rifle target practice was added at a shooting range developed on the east side of the former lake road. Torch Lake offered swimming, sailing, rowing, lifesaving, and rock collecting. At the waterfront was a long pier and a swimming platform in eight feet of water with a ten-foot diving platform. The woods offered hiking and camping. In the activities room beneath the New Lodge, we could pursue leather craft, woodworking, and a forge. Later on, a stone polishing tumbler appeared. We kept it busy polishing the Petoskey stones and colorful striped granite rocks from the beach. By my 3rd or 4th summer, I began to wonder why the supply of Petoskey stones was never exhausted, being collected by the dozens every summer.

There were plenty of marine fossils in the sedimentary rocks the winter ice brought in or exposed. Occasionally there were more exotic finds. I once found a small dinosaur footprint. It was an overgrown chicken-claw impression in a bluish-gray rock. I found it while skipping stones one afternoon. It was oval, flat and smooth. Fortunately, I turned it over before I threw it and discovered the imprinted claw mark. I kept it for many years in a tin cookie box with a few other trinkets and mementos — a horsemanship medal(!) from Fountain Valley, an autographed Charlie Gehringer baseball card from Uncle Jere on my 12th birthday, an inlaid silver belt buckle purchased on a Native American reservation in Colorado during my Fountain Valley days, two buttons from a WWI army uniform along with an AEF shoulder patch, and a small brass Packard script from my brother Trafton who had been a Packard dealer in Seattle. The cookie tin disappeared in the 1950s around the time of our move from Grosse Pointe to Rochester — a symbolic parting with Grosse Pointe life.

A popular woodworking project was constructing model yachts. I made increasingly improved sailboats over my first three summers, but my sailboats never had the sleek nautical shapes that the better carpenters and modelers achieved. Nonetheless, I enjoyed the informal races we had when we completed our boats, launching them from the swimming platform towards the pier. The third summer my boat even won one race — the high point of the summer and the end of my model yachting career.

The camp routine usually followed sunrise and sunset. Although the villages of Central Lake and Bellaire had electric power plants at the turn of the century, electricity rarely extended beyond the villages until the rural electrification projects in the 1930s. Electric power did not reach Hayo-Went-Ha until around 1940. Until then, lighting after dark was provided by kerosene lamps. The cabins did not have electric lights when I was a camper. Given the limited lighting, most activities ended at dark. The camp season began in late June, just after the summer solstice, and sunset was 9:30 p.m. with a twilight that hovered, gradually dimming for another hour. Eight weeks later as camp ended for the season, sunset had retreated to 8 p.m. and the twilight was shorter. As a result, six days a week, most activities at camp ended with "Taps," thirty minutes before sunset.

The last of the daylight was spent preparing for bed. It was a time of stories and songs in the cabins. Bill Dewey, a counselor in our cabin the first year, had been on the first Ontario canoe trip in 1932 and had a nearly inexhaustible fund of stories just from that trip. He had many other stories from his five years at camp. But he also read stories to us. I remember listening to *Robinson Crusoe* my first summer, doled out in 15-minute installments over four weeks.

Bill loved riddles and announced there would be a cabin riddle contest every Tuesday night. Riddle books were popular in the 1930s and a number circulated in the camp. By the end of the summer, we campers in Cabin 6 had found and memorized them all.

It was Cap's routine to visit two cabins each evening, permitting him to visit all the cabins during the week. His visits were usually the highlight of the day. He always had a story with a twist. Cap would make the opportunity to speak to each camper in the cabin, looking him in the eye with undivided attention, no matter how trivial the topic. It was our chance to tell him the things we had accomplished in the prior week, receiving compliments for "Great effort," "I saw how hard you were working," or "How well you were playing." A comment as simple as "How interesting" made us feel important. Often a camper's question or comment would prompt a short story from camp history, no doubt told a dozen times before, but always delivered as if Cap was sharing the story for the first time.

Songs and Stories

On Saturday evenings and ceremonial days, the best part of the day started after "Taps" when the entire camp gathered around a camp fire. That was the time for stories and songs, begun by Cap and taken up by staff, counselors and campers. There was an established canon we learned by heart over the years, and other songs and stories that were transitory, sometimes repeated for several summers, others heard only once.

There were two sets of camp songs, campfire songs and Sunday songs and hymns. The campfire songs were a mixture of traditional songs and popular tunes. A frequent song at sunset on the beach was Kate Smith's "God Bless America." We loved Cab Calloway's "Minnie the Moocher" and Gene Autry's "Back in the Saddle Again." Another song that comes to mind is "Indian Love Call" with Jeanette MacDonald and Nelson Eddy because it includes a yodel in the chorus that set us campers howling like wolves. We sang "Brother can you spare a dime" inspired by the tough economic times we were living in. In early 1940, Cap heard Woody Guthrie on the radio and brought "So Long, It's Been Good to Know You," "This Land is Your Land," and "Do Re Mi" to our campfires. Woody's songs often prompted brief remarks from Cap about our duty to our fellow man.

On Sunday, we sang "Angels Watching Over Me," "Swing Low Sweet Chariot," and "Wherever He Leads, I'll Go." In the late 1930s, the camp hymnal was expanded to include "Morning Has Broken," and "When the Saints Go Marching In." The benches in the outdoor chapel faced the lake through a gap in the trees framing Cap's lectern. "Morning Has Broken" often opened our Sunday service as the rising sun lit up the west shore of the lake behind Cap, while the "Saints" provided a rousing close as we headed for breakfast.

THE CAMP AND ITS TRADITIONS

We also had a Camp Yell:

Hey! Hey! Hey! Say! Say! Say!
We're the boys that have come to stay
We yell and yell from morn 'till night,
We've got a camp that's just all right,
The greatest camp you ever saw.
Hayo-Went-Ha Ha! Ha! Ha!

The canon of camp stories always began with "The Founders Three" and "The Ladle," told during each summer's first camp fire.

Cap always closed "The Founders Three" by saying that worthwhile things to improve the world, even great things, can be accomplished following three simple principles — a clear vision of the end sought (a camp where boys can grow to be men), a belief in the vision so strong it generates determination to accomplish that vision (hours of hiking to find the perfect place for the camp), and the knowledge that the combination of vision, belief, and determination will bring others to the cause (50 acres acquired in just one day), accomplishing great things.

Then with a wry smile, Cap reminded us these same principles applied to long camping trips in the rain and demanding chores at the camp or at home. "It is not the challenge," he would say, "but how we respond that makes us men and leaders."

While I first heard "The Founders Three" as a story about a long hike and a boat ride, it became, after a few summers, a parable of conviction and action to achieve a worthy goal. It stood me good stead on a Manistee canoe trip I will describe in a later chapter.

"The Ladle" served as the origin story for the camp's motto. For many years, the supply of drinking water came primarily from the spring-fed creek running through camp and next to the Old Dining Hall. The path from the athletic fields to the Old Dining Hall ran along the creek and at one location a ladle was hung from on overhanging cedar branch. One long hot afternoon devoted to baseball, as the returning players approached the Old Dining Hall, a race to the ladle ensued. The first thirsty boy who reached the creek grabbed the ladle and filled it to the brim with clear, cold water. Just as he was about to drink, the second boy arrived. The first camper, instead of drinking, passed the ladle to the second boy. And just as the second boy was about to drink the sweet water, another camper arrived. The second camper immediately passed the ladle on without drinking. This continued until the last boy arrived and he took the first drink. The story always closed with "Each for all and all for each."

What we first took away from these stories as junior campers often had been changed by our camp experiences by the time we became storytellers as counselors because the lessons in these stories had come alive through our experiences.

Thinking of those stories reminds me of one poem Cap recited every summer to our great delight, "The Cremation of Sam McGee" by Robert Service — the story of "The strange things done in the midnight sun by the men who moil for gold." The telling was reserved for the first chilly evening in August when there was a hint of autumn in the air. One summer its telling was prompted by a grand display of northern lights. That evening when Cap delivered the line, "The Northern Lights have seen queer sights, but the queerest they ever did see…," he paused, first looking up at the swirling green curtain in the sky above us and then around at the campers circling the fire, before continuing the poem. I swear an owl in the woods hooted during that moment. That dramatic effect produced a shiver down my spine in the darkness. I was not alone. By the third summer, I had committed that poem to memory.

Indian Council

The most important campfire ceremony, the Indian Council, took place at the end of the summer. The ceremony was nearly as old as the camp itself. All campers dressed in Native American gear, wrapped in blankets. We were led in single file to the Council Ring and sat in around an unlit campfire. The Council Ring was a circular fenced enclosure with a bench attached to the inside of the fence. At the north, west, and east quadrants were Hayo-Went-Ha's three totems: Tortoise, Wolf, and Bear, while the entrance to the ring was at the south quadrant. Four counselors dressed as Native American guides carried torches and led the procession of campers. Often there were fires on platforms along the way. The guides formed a square around the camp fire and the Chief (usually Cap) arrived by canoe from the lake. He joined Medicine Man facing the lake in front of the totem pole. The Chief began with a speech extolling the virtues of the tribes. Then the Medicine Man called on the Great Spirit to light the campfire. At his command, there would be a brief glow and then the campfire would burst into flame. In later summers, a flaming arrow came down for a tree to start the fire. One year, a prankster placed firecrackers among the kindling. They exploded in a series of bangs and sparks as the fire caught, creating a memorable council fire. The prankster was never identified.

Only after I came a counselor did I learn the secret to this magic. The fire was started with a separated mixture of sugar, sulfuric acid, and hydrochloric acid in a container. A trip wire was used to tip the container, mixing the contents and causing the fire. A guide pulled the trip wire at the right moment.

Each guide gave an oration about one quality: Courage, Honesty, Strength, and Wisdom. The Chief then described how brotherhood holds a tribe together. He closed with a request for counsel.

At that request, Hayo-Went-Ha appeared on the hill behind the totem pole and called on Ongue Hovie (Iroquois for "men surpassing all others") to join in brotherhood. His peroration would always end:

Brothers! Harken what I say!
Hayo-Went-Ha's words are good;
Union is our hope today.
All our hope in brotherhood!
If by this my counsel led,
Choose ye by tomorrow's sun;
Hayo-Went-Ha, he has said.
Hayo-Went-Ha he has done.

As the fire died, the Medicine Man gave his blessings and we returned in silence to our cabins.

THE CAMP AND ITS TRADITIONS

Mable at the Helena Dock[MSU]

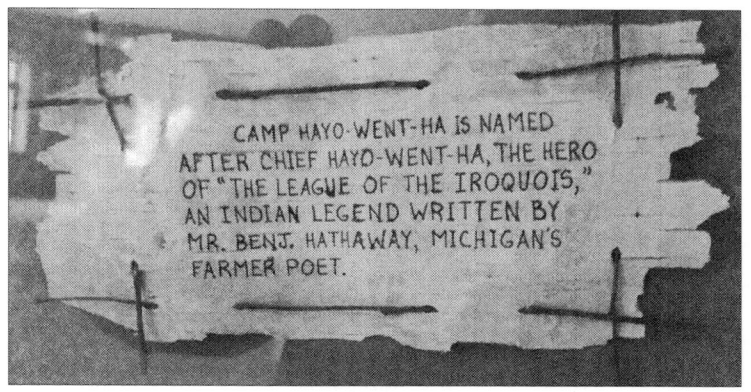

CAMP HAYO-WENT-HA IS NAMED AFTER CHIEF HAYO-WENT-HA, THE HERO OF "THE LEAGUE OF THE IROQUOIS," AN INDIAN LEGEND WRITTEN BY MR. BENJ. HATHAWAY, MICHIGAN'S FARMER POET.

HWH Birch Bark[HWH]

Boat House[HWH]

Boat House Carvings[HWH]

THE CAMP AND ITS TRADITIONS

Indian Council Ring[HWH]

Chapel[HWH]

Making Model Sailboats[HWH]

Each for All and All for Each[HWH]

THE CAMP AND ITS TRADITIONS

Open Air Dining Hall[HWH]

New (Bonbright) Lodge[HWH]

Cabin 6[A]

Boys in Workshop[HWH]

THE CAMP AND ITS TRADITIONS

Ladle at Spring[HWH]

Indian Chief and Guides[HWH]

TORCH LAKE SUMMERS

CHAPTER FIVE

The Mary Lou

The camp prided itself on its sailing program. There were three main & jib sailboats governed by the *Mary Lou*, as ungainly a 25-footer as ever sailed. She was ketch rigged, with patched sails and a tangle of rigging — four halyards, jack stays, jill stays, baby stays, runners, outhauls, uphauls (greater and lesser) and downhauls (lesser and greater), lifting tops and two-dozen other lines I never could memorize — rigging that provided a graduate course in knotting and splicing.

I never proved much of a student of the arcane nautical arts and still have this nightmare: I have gotten halfway through the litany of lines and rigging and then lost my place in front of the impatient stares of my crewmates, all of whom, at least in my dream, had rattled off the complete list, in alphabetical order no less.

The *Mary Lou* had a little cuddy cabin whose principal purpose, as far as I could tell, was to create a tiny sump area just above the keel, giving the smallest sailors access to the keel where bailing could be conducted with maximum efficiency. I had the dubious honor of being the smallest

TORCH LAKE SUMMERS

OLD TORCH IS BLUE.

10-year-old in camp in 1934. Standing my very tallest, I was a half inch shorter than Tommy Baldwin as summer began. My growth spurt in late July passed him by, but not in time to be recognized by most campers.

Unfortunately, from my perspective, Tommy was not a sailor. So, on that first summer, I had several opportunities to occupy that cramped, damp space at the bottom of the cuddy cabin and learn the peculiar backward swinging motion required to pass the bailing bucket up to the boys on the deck above and behind me. My bailing had such little effect I came to suspect my crew mates were not bothering to empty the bucket overboard but merely, in an economy of motion, dumping it on the deck before passing it back.

We were told the *Mary Lou* was a hundred years old and had plied the fur trade between Mackinac and Chicago. Older campers had been known to hide a beaver or muskrat skin under the deck, to be pulled out at an appropriate time to prove the story true. She had been hauled overland in the winter of 1907 from a port on East Bay to Torch Lake and pulled across the ice by a team of horses. Mid lake, the ice cracked. The horses were unhitched in time to save them but the *Mary Lou* sank through the ice until she floated, trapped in the ice. She was left, to be recovered when the ice went out. By late March, she had drifted with the ice nearly to Alden.

I recall a long tale, a saga in some tellings, of the sail back to camp through ice floes. Though credible at the time, with the passing of years I have begun to doubt the tale, particularly the part about a bear stranded on the ice attempting to board the *Mary Lou*.

No sailor would describe the *Mary Lou* as seaworthy. I am sure that was the reason she rarely sailed beyond swimming distance from shore. A medium breeze caused her to heel like a three-master in a gale. That created a great sense of adventure as well as seasickness in younger sailors.

By the time I arrived at camp, regardless of her real age, the *Mary Lou* was in her dotage. I sailed on her perhaps five times in the first two weeks at camp. Over the previous winter, Cap wisely concluded the *Mary Lou* was a potential maritime disaster. He had a flair for the dramatic and came up with a solution for her final sail. She was far too heavy to be beached and stripped. One night around a campfire Cap claimed he had researched the subject and learned of an Ojibway tradition. Chiefs who died in battle were sent out into Lake Michigan in a burning birchbark canoe. Well, Cap proposed, didn't the *Mary Lou* deserve a funeral with similar dignity?

So on the Fourth of July 1934, at dusk with the slightest of north breezes, she was cast adrift, her funeral fire encouraged by several gallons of kerosene soaking in her crumpled sails in the cuddy cabin. We had spent the day filling her with rocks, in the expectation that when the fire reached the waterline, she would swamp and the ballast would carry her 300 feet down.

But before she became a funeral pyre, we spent at least an hour with patriotic speeches, songs and stories. With an eye to the spectacular fire to come, the culminating stories involved tales of the surrender of Vicksburg and the victory at the Gettysburg, both on July 4, 1863. When the battle of Gettysburg ended, we stood at attention, faced the flag, and recited the pledge of allegiance. The camp cannon fired four times. At the command "About Face," we turned to face the lake and the *Mary Lou* moored just off shore.

The counselors cut cards to see who would get the honor of paddling out to the *Mary Lou* to cast her loose and then set her afire. But, the two counselors who cut the highest cards got the sequence wrong and started the fire before cutting her loose. The blaze erupted with a roar, surprising the counselors standing on the deck behind the flames. The counselors leapt the flames and scrambled to the bow to cut the mooring loose. Their canoe was swamped in the process and the counselors swam ashore. To add more excitement to the affair, the wind often eddies in the camp cove when it is from the north. For a moment, an eddy pushed the *Mary Lou* toward shore, prompting a great deal of shouting, "Get back," "Look out," etc. But after a minute, the north breeze caught her and she drifted south. An hour later, she was still floating south and fiercely blazing when *Taps* sounded and we headed to our cabins. Peaking through the cabin window, I could see the orange glow until I fell asleep. You can't imagine a better Fourth of July.

Forty years later, I visited the Hupp cottage in early July. Chatting about my camp experiences with Kay Hupp, I told the tale of the *Mary Lou*. She smiled. Nineteen thirty-four was her second summer at Torch. She had seen the *Mary Lou* float by, all ablaze. That caused as much excitement for her family as it had for the campers, and considerable speculation.

Kay knew the *Mary Lou*'s fate. She was more seaworthy than expected. She had drifted until the middle of the night, coming aground on Larsens Point, four miles down the lake where she had burned to the waterline. There wasn't much left of her when she was found in the morning by members of the Torch Lake Yacht and Country Club which is located on the point. They salvaged her keel and some planking. The keel was attached to the club dock as a bumper for several years. The planking was incorporated into a shed where garden equipment was kept. For a few years you could see her rock ballast in eight feet of water. Canoe trips down the lake always detoured for a view. By my last year at camp, the ice had erased that last trace of the *Mary Lou*.

TORCH LAKE SUMMERS

Boys on the *Mary Lou*[HWH]

***Mary Lou*, July 4, 1934[HWH]**

CHAPTER SIX

FRIENDSHIP

I turned 14 as I started my fifth summer at Hayo-Went-Ha. It was a busy, happy time but, per Cap's advice, when summer ended I took only one day away with me to keep forever.

Most of the area around the camp had been replanted with pine in the 1920s, all but a five-acre field still in need of trees. The camp received a WPA forestry grant to expand the pine planting to that field. I remember 1938 as a long summer because we campers spent several weeks planting that godforsaken field.

We planted two rows each morning and took the afternoon off for regular camp activities. When your job is planting a seedling every 10 feet, a row 2,000 feet long seems endless. We worked in pairs. One camper had a small shovel and dug the hole. The other camper carried a satchel with seedlings. He stooped and planted one in every hole. Dig, stoop, plant; dig, stoop, plant. Everyone hated stooping and planting; backs began to ache within 10 minutes of that labor. The tacit understanding was that the jobs would be traded halfway along the row.

THE TOTEM POLE.

FRIENDSHIP

Each pair started with 400 seedlings and a jug of water. We began at 8 a.m. before the sun was up high, hoping to finish before it got too hot. The field was open and shadeless. The sandy soil radiated heat. We made good progress the first hour. But the higher the sun got, the hotter we got and the longer the row became. We had a break every hour, the shortest five minutes I had ever experienced. It took over two hours to get to the end of the row and another two to plant the return row.

The project started on the fourth week of camp. I remember the first day. Tommy Baldwin and I paired up. We had become good friends since we met as new campers on the train to camp in 1934. We drank all our water long before we reached the turn at the end of the first row. By then we were thirsty and sunburned.

Our friendship of five summers nearly ended halfway back on the second row when Tommy refused to give me the shovel and take over the stooping and planting. Angry words had become a fist fight by the time a counselor pulled us apart. We did not speak for the next hour as we finished the row, or during the walk back to camp, or during lunch and dinner.

As we left the dining area after dinner, Cap took us aside and suggested we walk to the bench at the point. Sitting on the bench, you could see fourteen miles to the south end of the lake. Although the most beautiful spot anywhere on Torch Lake, it was not a focus of camp activities. We campers were far too busy to sit and enjoy the view. As we walked to the point in silence, my feelings were divided between outrage at Tommy and a deep sense of trepidation. I could think of only one other fist fight. Cap had threatened both boys with being sent home in disgrace and confined them to their cabins for three days.

Cap was rightly revered by campers, counselors and staff. He had a strong presence, quietly exercised. He always found the right thing to say, something that captured the values of the YMCA, something that helped us find humor and strength in challenging situations, something that gave us a perspective much larger than our own limited view.

No one spoke as we walked to the point and now, with the sun low in the west, the silence continued. The lake was still, the day breeze had died away and the cool evening breeze had not yet begun.

Cap took the middle of the bench and we sat on either side. He knew both of us well because it was our fifth summer. Cap knew Tommy and I were good friends. He did not ask us what the fight was about. He understood stoop labor, hot sun and thirst would try even the best of friendships. Instead, Cap began by asking Tommy about the eight-day canoeing trip on the Manistee River we had completed the week before.

Clarence had trucked us to a point where we had put our canoes in. It would take seven days to paddle down to the town of Manistee, camping along the way. We planned to spend the last night camped on the beach at Lake Michigan. The Manistee was full of snags in those days, long before the canoe livery services and conservation projects helped clear the river to help recreational canoeing.

Tommy and I had shared a canoe. On the second day in the middle section of the Manistee, the current is strong and there were many snags. We were in the trailing canoe. Three hours into the trip, an eddy in the current carried our canoe under an overhanging tree trunk where it became stuck. In attempting to unjam the canoe, we flipped it. Tommy's shirt collar caught on a low overhanging branch and it held him, head upstream, feet downstream, with his head barely above the water. The current was carrying water over his head and he was having a hard time catching his breath. The canoe had become firmly jammed between the fallen tree and the bank. I scrambled to the bank and crawled out on the fallen trunk. Between me pulling from above and Tommy wiggling below, he slid out of his shirt to freedom. I could not free his shirt.

The rest of our party was around a bend when we flipped the canoe and continued downriver, no doubt thinking Tommy and I were taking our own sweet time.

Together, we righted the canoe, hauled our gear to the bank and emptied the canoe. One paddle floated to the bank near the canoe but the other disappeared downstream. It took 20 minutes to force the canoe upstream from the wedge created by the bank and the fallen trunk, with one of us in the water pushing and the other fending off from the trunk. When we finally freed the canoe, the current caught it. Tommy, who was in the water, was just able to grab the stern. Somehow, he maneuvered the canoe to the opposite bank downstream. We spent long minutes loading our gear back into the canoe, all the while waist deep in the cold Manistee. By the time we were ready to continue, we were cold, wet, and exhausted 14-year-old boys with a three-hour paddle to the next camp site.

Those three hours were a nightmare. One of us paddled and steered from the back while the other in front pushed the canoe around snags. As we weaved downstream, one snag then another caught the canoe. Sometimes, one of us had to jump out of the canoe to free it. Part way along, we pulled into the bank and, after a 10-minute search, found a long straight branch to help us pole around obstructions. When we reached the camp site an hour later, we were scratched and bruised, and shivering with cold and sunburn. But we knew we could count on each other, thick or thin. The rest of the trip, thank heavens, was uneventful.

The telling of the tale took time. Although Tommy started the narration, it soon became a joint effort. Cap asked just enough questions to bring out a few details and help us relive that day in full. The sun was touching the hill across the lake when our story ran down and silence returned.

After a long, quiet minute or two, Cap broke the silence. "Boys, you have two days you can remember forever from this summer, one that shows you at your best and one that shows you at your worst. One day you took care of each other, the other you did not. I know you both. I know which day you will choose to remember. Now stand up and shake hands." We stood up and shook hands. Cap said, "Time for you boys to head up to camp. I think I will enjoy the view a while longer."

"Taps" sounded as Tommy and I walked up the stairs from the beach, our friendship cemented. We remained campers and best friends through the summer of 1942.

FRIENDSHIP

Canoeing on the Manistee River[HWH]

The Bench on Tyler's Point[RB]

TORCH LAKE SUMMERS

CHAPTER SEVEN

Drums

The summer of 1939, the summer that transformed me, started slowly. I finished 9th grade at GUPAS, a lackluster school year where my best grade was a C in algebra, followed by a D in English and an F in Latin. My mother made clear during the school year there was no point paying for a private school education on a straitened budget if I was not prepared to work hard. And I had not been prepared to work hard. So, I was off to a new school, Grosse Pointe High, and a new set of friends to look forward to in the fall.

In the spring of 1939, Charlie Neff invited me to come along on his family's six-week trip to France. My mother would not agree after considering the tight family budget, her lack of interest in rewarding my dismal academic performance, and concern with the political situation in Europe — all reasons I found unpersuasive. She insisted I return to Hayo-Went-Ha.

I had had five summers, albeit wonderful ones, at Hayo-Went-Ha, but another summer on Torch seemed tame compared to six weeks in England and France. I could

NEW BONBRIGHT LODGE.

not forsee that four years later I would begin an extended all-expense-paid tour of England and the continent, courtesy of the U.S. Army. Hayo-Went-Ha was second best in my eyes.

I was reconciled to my summer plans when Uncle Jere gave me the now traditional lunch on the way to the Michigan Central train station. I shared with him the injustice of being forced to pass up a once-in-a-lifetime experience, emphasizing that the trip would cost my mother little more than round trip Atlantic passage. Uncle Jere lent a sympathetic ear but made sure I boarded the sleeping car at 5 p.m., as always with two sandwiches and a piece of cake in my knapsack. I expect that before we changed trains in Grand Rapids my summer pals were tired of my complaints about the summer I could have had.

Being the age I was, shortly after my arrival at Hayo-Went-Ha I even explained to Cap that, while the camp was fine, there were more interesting places for a 15-year-old boy to spend his summer. I got no sympathy from him. Instead I received a sermon about bucking up, followed by the compliment he was looking forward to seeing me put all my camp experience to work as a new junior counselor. The smell of the cedars, the ice-cold water of Torch, the fabulous blue water stretching south to the hills miles away, and the stories told amid the smoke of the summer's first camp fire did much to restore my mood, but even then, a little regret and resentment lingered.

That summer Cap expanded camp activities to include music and the arts. I did not yet fancy myself a singer and my piano lessons in fifth grade lasted only five weeks before my piano teacher and I, by agreement, parted company. So, when Cap announced a musical talent contest for the first week of August, I did not give it a thought.

I went on a three-week trip in the U.P. after July 4th. Tommy and I had had little opportunity to spend much time together before I left on the trip. When I returned near the end of July, Tommy approached me with a strange proposition. He had entered the musical talent contest, pairing up with Toby Randall, a trumpet player. Toby had succeeded Karl as Hayo-Went-Ha's bugler. Tommy and Toby entered the contest as a trio but were short a drummer. Tommy thought I should become their drummer.

Tommy played the clarinet and brought it to camp with him. I heard him play once or twice. In the 1920s and 1930s, Detroit had a thriving jazz scene including many notable clarinetists. Tommy was interested in music from an early age and had heard many classical and jazz performances. Tommy had not heard Benny Goodman perform in Detroit, but when Goodman joined the NBC radio program, *Let's Dance*, in early 1934, Tommy claimed him as Detroit's own and became his biggest fan.

For reasons not clear then or now, Cap suggested to Tommy that I might agree to be the drummer. That may have resulted from my habit (regarded as a bad habit by my family) of tapping absentmindedly when either bored or occupied on a project. Possibly Cap heard something in that tapping beyond an annoying distraction.

Regardless, Tommy, desperate for a drummer and with the contest just three weeks away, asked me to be his drummer. After 30 minutes of cajoling, I agreed. Tommy assured me drumming was as easy as breathing; anybody could do it. Which turned out to be true, at least for me.

Although the trio now had a drummer, there remained the matter of a drum. Cap had a vague recollection that a camper brought a drum to camp in 1930 or '31 and encouraged us to look for it. Rummaging around one shed at the camp, we found a snare drum beneath a tarp and hidden behind a broken wheelbarrow, parts for a Model T, and an assortment of old farm tools. Further excavation in the back corner of the shed yielded one drum stick. After another dusty hour searching in other sheds, we found nothing more. Tommy, although unimpressed with what we found, reluctantly conceded it would have to do.

We needed a cymbal. Negotiations with the cook produced a cymbal in the form of a lid for an old two-gallon cooking pot. I was charged with cleaning up the snare drum, mounting our cymbal on an improvised stand and whittling another drumstick.

Rehearsals began the next day. We had ten days to rehearse. Fortunately for me, one of the senior counselors played the drum and gave me my first lessons. In the camp schedule, midafternoon was free time if you were not on a trip. We began our efforts in the New Lodge but, after our first practice session, others in the building begged us to practice elsewhere. A campfire circle along the northern edge of the camp property became our rehearsal space. A flock of crows lived in the high pines and always flew off in noisy protest when our practice began. As the date of the talent contest approached, our catch phrase became, "At least the audience won't be a bad as the crows."

Tommy's musical expectations for a jazz number featuring a clarinet solo inspired by his hero Benny Goodman quickly confronted reality. Even the great Gene Krupa did not beat out a syncopated jazz rhythm his first week on the drums and Toby's trumpet experience was strictly classical.

Tommy and Toby conferred, argued and negotiated over a suitable piece of music that would highlight, at least in Tommy's mind, his talent on the clarinet. He argued for a snappy Goodman tune he heard on *Let's Dance* but we settled on Harold Arlen's "It's Only a Paper Moon," a popular tune in four/four time that demanded little of Toby or me. In later years, Ella Fitzgerald's renditions of this song always took me back to three boys in short pants practicing in the woods with squirrels and crows for an audience.

With a simple tune and four/four time, our little trio came together and, considering the circumstances, reached a creditable performance level. We got through our performance without a hitch, although my crude percussion equipment drew a few catcalls as we set up. Toby's cabin mates had heard the crow story, and, amid the applause, we heard a few "Caw, Caw, Caws." Although Tommy had ambitions of winning the amateur contest, we did not win, place or show.

I did not join the trio to seek instant fame; satisfaction with our performance after a few rehearsals was enough for me. I was relieved to have the ordeal of my first public performance behind me. There is no tougher audience than fellow campers. In some ways, the performance did not matter. I had fallen in love with music in general and the drums in particular. For the last two weeks of camp, we took on two more pieces of music and my drumming lessons continued. I could not wait to get home to get a proper drum set and to listen to *Let's Dance* on WXYZ.

Over the winter, I convinced (badgered) my mother into buying me a drum set. She held out for several months but gave in at Christmas. She banished me to the garage behind our house on Lincoln to practice. I spent the winter of 1939/40 sharing my rehearsal space with the family's dark blue 1932 Buick.

CHAPTER EIGHT
CANOE TRIPS

Hayo-Went-Ha canoe trips were always memorable. Three come to mind besides the 1937 Manistee River trip with Tommy Baldwin.

1936 — MANISTEE RIVER

There are several abandoned Ottawa camp or village sites along the Manistee River. On my first canoeing trip on the Manistee in 1936, we camped at one on a low hill within a broad 180-degree bend in the river. Our counselor was an archeology major and knew a great deal about former Native American settlements in Michigan. He identified several former sites along the Manistee and planned our daily progress to overnight at them when convenient. Evenings around the campfire, he filled our heads with tales of Ottawa lore. On the quiet river under the starlight, peering at the dim faces of our party in the firelight, we imagined we were a band of Ottawa traveling down the river carrying bundles of pelts to trade with the white man along the Lake Michigan shore. We made up a canoeing chant and sang it into the darkness.

The next morning, we spent two hours looking for arrowheads, ax heads, and pottery shards. Rafe Merrill struck gold, as it were, and found three arrow points. We concluded the reddish staining on the points was blood — although the more likely explanation was iron staining from the many seeps along the river. Art Townsend found a tin cup and decided it was at least 100 years old, left behind by French traders on a trip up the river. But, when Art cleaned the cup back at camp, he found "Sears Roebuck & Co. 1923" stamped on the bottom. As always, our imaginations outpaced reality — but that is what turns long days of paddling and hot sun or rain into cherished lifetime memories. I suspect when Rafe and Art told their children and grandchildren the story of that canoeing trip, the romance of the finds survived, and any conflicting facts were lost in the passage of time.

1939 – Tahquamenon River and Lake Superior

My first year as a junior counselor was notable not only for the beginning of my romance with drumming but also a demanding three-week canoe trip in the Upper Peninsula. Clarence drove Tom Willetts as senior counselor and me as the junior counselor with ten campers and six canoes to the Tahquamenon River near Newberry. We paddled down the river and portaged around Upper and Lower Tahquamenon Falls. It took five days to reach Lake Superior at Whitefish Bay. The river enters Lake Superior about three miles from Paradise. Two campers and I hiked into town and called the camp to report our arrival. We bought as many provisions as our backpacks would hold and hiked back to the river. The rest of the expedition made camp. We celebrated the completion of the first leg of our journey with an impromptu war dance.

In the morning, we turned east and began the long second leg along the shore of Whitefish Bay. Our destination was Sault Ste. Marie. There was almost no development on the south shore of Lake Superior, so it was easy to imagine we were fur traders 300 years ago. We enjoyed a day of perfect canoeing weather, then storms and wet weather set in. We took three more days to reach Dollar Settlement at the eastern end of Whitefish Bay, two days behind schedule. Along the way we swamped several canoes and spent three nights camping in the rain. On the bright side, the miserable weather cut down on the black flies that plagued us on the Tahquamenon River.

As a counselor, at the end of every day in good or awful weather I was responsible for helping campers beach their canoes and set up their tents. I took the lead in making one of the two campfires and organizing the meals. I needed to read the spirits of my campers and find the right words to restore morale when needed — and moral boosting was needed during that miserable week on Lake Superior. Whenever a camper's canoe swamped, I jumped in the water to help right it and gather up any possessions or supplies floating away. I stayed in the water until the campers and equipment wer back in the canoe and ready to go on. By god, Lake Superior was cold — colder than a well digger's ass!

Dollar Settlement was the first sign of human habitation we had seen in three days. We spotted a wide beach and what appeared to be a permanent track up the face of a steep bluff. I hiked up the bluff but saw only cutover scrub. As I turned to return to the expedition on the beach, I saw overhead wires and followed them to the small, one-room general store. As I hoped, the store had a telephone. It took a while but eventually the operator connected me with the camp. Aware of the storms on Lake Superior, Cap was glad to hear my report that all campers were well, if wet and cold. He listened to my tale of swamped canoes and angry storms. He told me, "I knew you and Tom could handle any difficulties you faced. I would not have sent you men as counselors if I had a moment's doubt."

After consultation, Cap dispatched Clarence with the truck to pick us up and transport us to Sault Ste. Marie to begin the last leg of our trip. Ever the optimist, Cap assured me some of the finest hiking trails in the U.P. were nearby and we should amuse ourselves hiking until Clarence arrived. Cap greatly overstated the quality of the hiking near Dollar Settlement and we were relieved when Clarence appeared at lunchtime on the second day. The storms and rain ended the day before and we had dried out and warmed up after a miserable week. Before Clarence arrived, we were already packed up and had lugged our gear and canoes up the bluff. Bouncing in the back of the truck on the two-track road from Dollar Settlement seemed luxurious compared to paddling on the big lake in constant fear of swamping.

Clarence took us to St. Marys River above the Soo Locks. After some discussion, the lock tenders permitted our canoes to pass through the locks with a 500-foot iron ore freighter. I had doubts about the idea but I mustered enough enthusiasm to help convince the lock tenders, Clarence and the more timid campers. Descent as the water sank in the lock involved equal measures of excitement and fright. The trick was controlling the position of the canoes to avoid getting squashed by the freighter, all while fighting the swirling currents within the lock induced by the draining water. The lock walls loomed 25 feet over our heads and we just glimpsed Clarence peering over the edge, hoping he would not have to call Cap and report he had lost a canoe and two campers to a collision with a freighter. We emerged from the lock safe and sound and excited by the experience.

Clarence wished us good speed as we set out on the third stage of our trip, Sault Ste. Marie to De Tour Village where the St. Marys River enters Lake Huron. We had a week of great weather and met Clarence on schedule late on a Wednesday afternoon. We camped at De Tour Village and then spent a long day driving back to the camp, crossing the Straits on the ferry from St. Ignace to Mackinaw City.

When we got back to camp, Jim Martin, the oldest of the ten campers on the trip, told Cap, "The trip was miserable and hard; it was the greatest time I ever had." Although this trip was a powerful experience for me because I practiced the leadership learned from others in prior summers, I had had enough canoeing for a lifetime. But, that was not to be the case.

1940 - Return to the Manistee

I left for camp with relief in June 1940. My 10th grade at Grosse Pointe High was only a slight improvement over 9th grade at GPUS but nothing to be proud of. My only scholastic highlight was joining the school's choir program. Both my mother and my teachers told me I was smart enough to get As and Bs but was failing to put the effort in. That was true.

On return from camp in August 1939, I convinced my mother to buy a set of drums for me when I told her how much fun I had in Tommy's trio. I then applied my time improving my skills as a drummer, not to my schoolwork. Frankly, I didn't care about school and happily put 250 miles between my disappointed mother and me when I headed off to camp.

Cap named me the senior counselor for the eight-day Manistee canoe trip. He paired me with Jim Martin who had graduated to junior counselor and had performed well on the Lake Superior trip. I was not crazy about the assignment, but I could hardly say "No" when Cap explained he chose me because I proved I could handle anything while on the Lake Superior trip. I expected no particular difficulties. This would be my third time down the Manistee, so I knew the river and campsites well.

We packed up on a Sunday afternoon and loaded the truck. We got off to an early start on a beautiful morning on the third week of July, usually the best weather of the summer. As the senior counselor, I rode shotgun in the cab with Clarence. The two-hour trip to the Manistee was a pleasure. Although this was my seventh summer, Clarence still had stories I had never heard.

The good weather lasted for one day, but the first challenge arrived before the weather turned. We entered the river in the middle of nowhere and paddled to a campsite just west of a county road. We took it easy the first day and arrived at the campsite about 5 p.m., plenty of time to make camp and cook dinner. As we unpacked the tents and camp gear, I asked Jim Martin where he had stowed the cooking gear. He reminded me I had agreed to pick up the equipment from the dining hall and, he said, "Apparently, that's where it still is." What to do, with 10 hungry campers and a hungry junior counselor staring at me? There was no point blaming Jim or anyone but myself, and not much point in that. I knew leaders acted, not complained.

The answer I came up with was to walk back to the county road, climb the embankment, walk to the nearest farmhouse, and see what cooking equipment I could borrow. But our problem would not be solved by borrowing; we had a seven-day trip ahead of us and needed cooking equipment every day. I would have to convince people to give us their cooking utensils with no hope of return. I felt a mixture of anger at my stupidity and embarrassment for having to ask for charity. I felt I had already disapointed Cap. But there was nothing left to do but start on my quest for cooking equipment.

I stopped at the top of the embankment to get my emotions under control. I don't know where the thought came from, but the Founders Three on Tyler's Point came to mind. They knew what they needed to do and their belief in their cause carried them many miles over significant obstacles to achieve their vision. And they got dinner and a roof overhead for the night as a bonus at the end of their quest. Well, I wasn't trying to buy hundreds of acres and found a summer camp, I only needed a few pots and pans and I most certainly would not have to hike 20 miles to accomplish that. And, like the Funders Three, there would be a hot meal as a reward at the end of a successful quest. So, with one camper for company, I set off down the road in a better frame of mind.

We reached a farm house in less than a quarter mile; it was just beyond a bend in the road. The woman who came to the door was surprised to see us but could not have been nicer. I stumbled through my explanation and request and was honest enough to say it would be my fault if my campers went hungry because I did not get any pots and pans. She contributed a two-quart pot and a ladle to our cause and told us the next farm was a ten-minute walk down the road.

There were two farms on either side of the road at that

point. The first one had a large white dog chained in the yard, but we screwed up our courage and sidled past. The farmer was not sympathetic, but his wife was helpful and provided other utensils. We struck it rich at the last farmhouse. The woman gave us the rest of the basic utensils we needed and a basket filled with raspberries to take with us.

We were back at the campsite 90 minutes after we set out. Jim had had more confidence in my cadging abilities than I, because when we returned he had two campfires going and food for dinner laid out on top of an overturned canoe.

The weather turned during the afternoon of the second day and a four-day rainstorm began. We pitched camp just before the rain began in the hope the storm would quickly pass. We spent the rest of the afternoon in our tents. The rain cleared up just long enough to cook dinner and then began again. It rained off and on all night. It was still raining in the morning with no sign of let up. We had to meet Clarence in six days, so we figured out how to use the tents and tent poles to create a crude lean-to on each canoe and set off in the rain. What followed were the three wettest days in my life. Fortunately, the weather was warm, but we never had a dry moment. On two days it was too wet to start a fire and we dined on cold rations.

To raise our spirits, I got everyone singing. We started with every campfire song and camp hymn we could remember. Then each canoe was challenged to make up a song and then another one. Then we sang hymns again and reprised the campfire songs. The time passed pretty well. The last two days, the weather changed and the rain stopped. The sun was shining when we spotted the camp truck at our rendezvous point.

Clarence bought us hot lunches at the first town we passed. He heard the saga of the "pots and pans crusade," as it became known. His only comment when I joined him in the truck's cab after lunch was, "I bet that's the last time anyone goes canoeing with you," and then he started to laugh.

Tahquamenon Falls Portage[HWH]

Canoes in Soo Locks[HWH]

CHAPTER NINE
FOUNTAIN VALLEY SCHOOL

My mother had planned to send me away to boarding school for high school — my older sisters and brother had gone out east to school — but family finances were tight in 1939 when I entered high school. After a dismal 9th grade at GUPAS and only slightly better performance in 10th grade at Grosse Pointe High, my mother sought and found another option.

I don't recall how she learned of the Fountain Valley School of Colorado. In the first week of September 1940, she not only convinced them to accept me but also wrangled a scholarship. So, on short notice I was sent out west to boarding school in Colorado Springs for my own good. Her hope was in that environment I would apply myself and live up to my potential. As my mother explained to Fountain Valley's headmaster in urging my acceptance, "David has a very good mind, and could do a lot better work than he has ... [but] so many outside interests, the school work suffers." She hoped that "in boarding school that is not so apt to be the case." No truer words were ever spoken about my approach to high school, but my mother was hoping in vain that Fountain Valley would focus my academic efforts. As I boarded the train and began my trip into what I saw as exile, my one consolation was I could bring my drum set to school.

Elizabeth Hare, a New Yorker who came to Colorado Springs in 1927, founded Fountain Valley School. She intended to create a school modeled on the prestigious schools in the east. She found support from a local philanthropist. In 1929 they purchased the Lazy B Ranch owned by Palm Beach polo enthusiast Jack Bradley. Besides a large main building, the ranch included a polo field, stables, and small residences for ranch hands. The school opened as a boarding school for boys in September 1930. Given its origin, Fountain Valley emphasized equestrian programs, although there were a variety of other sports.

I was placed in Fourth Form and had thirteen classmates. My first semester was not an academic success. My tutor evaluated me, "Full mark below bogey. Should do much better." As the Headmaster wrote to my mother in December, my work was a "terrible disappointment;" I had achieved "one of the lowest records in the School." My tutor put his finger on the cause of my downfall, "His keen drumming a great attraction — but spends too much time on it."

Since I had not wanted to be there at all, I graded the semester on my other activities and felt it had been successful and productive. I had gone on a five-day camping trip on Pikes Peak during my third week of school. Given my years of camping experience at Hayo-Went-Ha, I had been a leader on the trip, earning the respect and friendship of the other boys. Inspired by my half-brother Leo who played on the University of Michigan's football teams in the late 1890s, I joined the football team and had fun on the field, despite being the smallest on the team. I had permission to visit Colorado Springs on the weekend, just a mile and a half from school. I also joined the Chorale Society and clearly enjoyed it — the only photo of me at Fountain Valley in which I am smiling! Best of all, I had a part in the fall play.

Theater saved me that fall. My interest in theater began

when I first met Shakespeare in my sophomore English literature class at Grosse Pointe High. We chose a sonnet to learn and then recite in class; my choice was "Sonnet 18," "Shall I compare thee to a Summer's day?" I can recite the whole sonnet still and am always touched by the first line — maybe because my image of an ideal summer's day includes the deep blue and aquamarine waters of Torch Lake. I loved to learn the lines and perfect the delivery needed to make "Sonnet 18" ring true. Later that year we read *Hamlet* and *A Midsummer Night's Dream*.

In the spring of 10th grade, I was cast in a minor role in the Grosse Pointe High School Pointe Players' production of *What a Life*, a play set in the principal's office of Central High School. I had just one line but, no matter how minor the part, I was hooked.

My goal for 11th grade at Grosse Pointe High was to be cast in a leading role in the fall play. I saw no reason to change that goal when I was exiled to Fountain Valley.

The Fountain Valley fall play was Andre Obey's *Noah*. I got a part but not the leading role. I played Japheth. That encouraged my ambitions for the stage. The script has roles for Mrs. Noah and for three girls who serve as companions to Noah's sons. The script describes the girls as "beautiful" and "well-formed." Tryouts were open to girls from the Colorado Springs high school. I would describe the casting of the girls as a success on both counts. Rehearsals with them cured me of my stage fright vis-à-vis the fairer sex.

In October 1940, Gilbert & Sullivan's *The Sorcerer* was announced as the spring musical, to be performed in March 1941. I immediately read the script and decided I wanted the part of the sorcerer, John Wellington Wells. In the first scene, a character asks Wells to give him a magic potion to win the heart a girl. Predictably, things go awry. The love potion is drunk by everyone and mismatched pairings occur. Everything is put to right in the last scene when the sorcerer is consumed in a flash of fire.

I studied the part from late October. Believe it or not, by auditions in the second week of January I had memorized not only the sorcerer's part, but almost the entire play. I was prepared to live up to my potential for the theater.

My second semester began better on the academic front. I was permitted to try out for the play on condition that I apply myself to academics. So I buckled down in January and February to earn my reward. I got the part of John Wellington Wells.

John Wellington Wells introduced Gilbert & Sullivan's first patter song. I remember the opening lines.

> Oh!
> My name is John Wellington Wells,
> I'm a dealer in magic and spells,
> In blessings and curses,
> And ever filled purses,
> In prophecies, witches, and knells.

Because Fountain Valley was a small school, actors assisted in all aspects of play production — costumes, set design and construction, props, and lighting. I loved putting on the sorcerer's makeup. I painted my face red and dyed my hair black. I perfected twisting the curly hair at the corners of my forehead into devil's horns. I added a black goatee to complete the effect. As a grownup, to my children's delight, I used every party involving costumes to reprise my sorcerer makeup, set off by my Grosse Pointe society tuxedo and tails.

The best part was rehearsals. Bringing the script alive requires both individual and group effort. I loved working to get it right, revealing the depths in the material that a solitary reading does not disclose. The process has always brought me an immense amount of satisfaction.

All this led up to the night of the performance — the apprehension before the curtain rose each night, the rhythm of the performance, the thrill of audience's reactions, and the high of the applause at the end.

At Fountain Valley, musicals were performed for three nights, Thursday to Saturday. Attendance on Thursday was limited to students and staff, but open to the public on Friday and Saturday. Colorado Springs was the county seat with a population then of 35,000, insuring we would have at least modest audience. I remember a sea of faces on the Friday and Saturday performances of *The Sorcerer*, but I am sure that reflected the first four or five rows within the reach of the footlights. Who knows how many were sitting in the dark rows beyond.

When *The Sorcerer* closed, I slacked off and returned my attention to my drums and other nonacademic pursuits. I am embarrassed now to recall how rude I was in this period to several of my teachers. My high school years were tough for me and for most of the grown-ups around me.

Boys at Fountain Valley School[FVS]

Fountain Valley School 4th Form[FVS]
Dave, First Row, Sixth from Left End

FOUNTAIN VALLEY SCHOOL

Fountain Valley School Glee Club[FVS]
Dave, Front Row, Right End

Noah Production[FVS]
Dave, Upstage Center

Dave as John Wellington Wells, *Sorcerer*[A]

CHAPTER TEN

SUMMER ROMANCE

Camp structure was a great thing. It kept our days organized, and it gave us challenges to work around. Now that I am much older, I realize Cap knew most of what happened at camp before and after dark, but we counselors operated in the naïve belief that what we did after dark was unseen and therefore unknown.

Kurt "Oak" Coakley was a year older than I and from Birmingham. He acquired the nickname Oak based on his broad shoulders and sturdy form. His sister Alice attended Four-Way Lodge, less than a mile down the shore from Hayo-Went-Ha. For several years Oak filled our heads with stories from the girls camp with his sister credited as the source. On more mature reflection, I think Oak made up at least half the stories, but they sounded interesting to me and other counselors.

The stories were all the more alluring because we could see the girls swimming off the Four-Way dock and swimming platform. There were occasional meetings on the lake between sailors and canoeists from both camps. But, other than good-natured ribbing in both directions, there was little to remember about the encounters. Hayo-Went-Ha guys were generally shy around girls, although there were a few big talkers, Oak among them.

Once a summer there was a "social" with Four-Way Lodge for the junior and senior counselors at each camp — always on the girls' territory. There were about 30 girls and 30 boys at the social. Four-Way Lodge had a large gathering space, an open-air building with screened sides. I think it served as the dining hall, like the former open dining hall at Hayo-Went-Ha.

I remember my first social in 1939, the year I became a junior counselor, as an awkward event where I stood inconspicuously at the edge of the dining hall, talking to my Hayo-Went-Ha friends. Several times during the social there were dances in which every boy or girl had to choose a partner. As one of the youngest, shortest and shyest, I was usually the last to choose or be chosen. Mostly we 15-year-olds watched the "world-wise" older counselors dance and flirt with the older girls.

The 1940 social was much the same, largely a spectator event, though I spent a little time chatting with a girl named Barbara. She was from Grand Rapids. I did my best to impress her with stories of social life in Grosse Pointe and my sisters as debutantes.

The summer of 1941 after my first year at Fountain Valley was different. I had just turned 17 and become extremely aware of girls. My theater experience with the girls in the casts of *Noah* and *The Sorcerer* gave me a certain amount of confidence with the fairer sex. With considerable interest I looked forward to the Four-Way Lodge social.

I was a canoeing instructor that summer and my flotilla had a surprising number of encounters on the lake with our counterparts from Four-Way. There was at least one paddle-splashing water fight between my flotilla and the Four-Way's fleet. The encounters became a running joke with Tommy Baldwin and Ben Harmon. They called me Pirate Dave and asked when I was going to board the girls' canoes, capture them and bring them back to camp. With my 17-year-old's confidence, I swelled in the kidding.

The camps were a mile apart, so true to Hayo-Went-Ha

form, we hiked to and from the social. We walked down at 6 p.m. and returned to camp after dark. On the appointed July evening in 1941, the overcast sky threatened rain and we were afraid we would arrive wet, looking like drowned rats. We hiked briskly and arrived a little out of breath. But the rain held off and by sunset the sky was clear, and we enjoyed a spectacular sunset.

Tommy Baldwin and I were intent on making a memorable impression. We convinced two other counselors to join us in an impromptu *a cappella* group for the social. The group learned two or three popular tunes and negotiated through Cap for the chance to perform at the social. We were sure our performance would be the path to conquest — conquest being, at most, the opportunity to monopolize a pretty girl and steal a kiss or two in the confusion accompanying the last 30 minutes of the social as the evening ended.

The evening could not have gone better. The first girl I saw on our arrival was Barbara. I can still remember, clear as day, how she looked when she turned from the refreshment table at the end of the dining hall and faced me. It took me a moment to recognize her from the prior summer. Barbara had also decided to make an impression at the social. In a navy and white horizontal-striped top with a navy high-waisted skirt and a matching blue beret, she was prettier than I remembered. Her outfit revealed her figure had filled out in all the right places. The first time I heard the lyrics to "Honey Bun," "Where she's narrow she's as narrow an arrow, And she's broad where a broad should be broad," that vision of Barbara came back.

Our glances met, and I literally was stopped in my tracks. Ben Harmon, behind me, tripped over me, giving me a push, and I staggered into the dining area. With that entrance, I was too embarrassed to go over and say Hello.

Our *a cappella* performance 20 minutes into the social was a great success, and we earned several admirers, including Barbara. Now I was a successful performer, not a stumbling boob. That was the beginning of a great evening.

Barbara and I started up where we had left off. I was more genuine and did not feel the need to tell Grosse Pointe society stories to impress her. I heard about school dances in Grand Rapids and her love of riding horses. One reason she attended Four-Way Lodge was its equestrian program. I told her about transferring to Fountain Valley School and the difficulty of making new friends a long way from home. While I described Fountain Valley was a "polo" school, I admitted I had no great love of horses, although to my surprise I had won a horsemanship award. Instead I had fallen in love with theater. Like me, Barbara had a part in her junior class play, so we had much to talk about. While I won't say I monopolized Barbara (not for lack of trying but other guys kept butting in to ask her to dance), we spent most of the evening talking and dancing.

While I had attended several dances in Grosse Pointe, they were stiff and formal affairs before I had discovered the allure of girls. Close, cheek-to-cheek dancing had not occurred on those occasions. I attribute my lifelong dislike of dancing to those dances.

This evening was different and so much better. The exuberance and joy of swing dancing are infectious. After a few awkward dances, we found our rhythm. Our feet and hips and arms and hands began to dance together. I found the more I focused on her eyes, the better I danced and the better we danced together. Then a slow number came on. This was nothing like those Grosse Pointe dances. The experience of having my arm around a girl, warm from the dancing, the pressure of her breasts against me, and close to her sparkling eyes — it was intoxicating to say the least. I was a little stiff to begin with, a holdover from those Grosse Pointe dances, but I soon got a grip on my subject and relaxed against her form. I can honestly say I never had another time like that on the dance floor.

The evening passed too quickly. I forget our subterfuge but around 9:30 I snuck out one side of the dining hall and she slipped out the other. There was a little twilight left, and the evening was warm. We sat under a cedar tree on a bank above the lake and watched a sliver of the moon setting in the west, pouring a silver streak across the lake.

I had never been alone with a girl under similar circumstances and for a moment lost my patter. A few inane comments about how swell the music was broke the ice. Soon we were laughing quietly about this and that.

As we sat side by side, we weren't quite shoulder to shoulder. Long agonized minutes passed while I tried to get my courage up to put my arm around her, all the while making distracted conversation. I knew I had only 30 minutes until the social ended at 10 p.m. and could feel the clock ticking. Barbara helped me out, perhaps she decided that without a little encouragement I would never make a romantic move, no matter how small. She suddenly gave a shiver and then leaned into me for warmth. My spontaneous reaction, to my surprise and relief, was to put my arm around her shoulder. I wasn't sure how much of a hug or a squeeze to give. I remember my arm getting tired as I tried not a release the full weight of my arm on to her shoulder. Thank god, I quickly tired and my arm curved around her naturally.

Then it was time to pluck up my courage again, this time for a kiss. The social always ended with the ringing of the camp bell at 9:50 p.m. As it began to ring, it was now or never. I found my courage and manage a clumsy kiss — my first. Looking back, Barbara's response seemed to show some experience. After that it was just a moment and a simultaneous movement by both of us for a second, real kiss. I remember bumping noses as we moved together. The third kiss was just right. Then, we heard voices rousing campers out of the shadows, and we made our way back to the lighted periphery of the dining hall.

This was the prelude to the great adventure of 1941.

As I mentioned, Oak's sister Alice was a Four-Way Lodge camper, a year older than Oak. Oak had met a girl, Jane, who caught his fancy. Like Barbara and me, they had spent time alone. Oak was a man of action. They had agreed at the first opportunity they would have an after-hours meeting. I forget what the signal was to be, but it was something Oak could see from the Boat House.

Oak had seen that I had found a girl. On the hike back to camp, Oak grabbed me by the elbow and pulled me to the back of the troop. He began, "Dave, who was that girl? She sure was cute." He quickly enlisted me in his plan to canoe down to the girls' camp after hours for a rendezvous with Jane. Oak explained he was sure I would want another opportunity to get together with Barbara and suggested I join him in the canoe. Of course, I answered, "Yes." He told me he had expected my answer and had primed Jane to enlist Barbara.

Every afternoon that week Oak spent the hour from 4 to 5 peering toward the girls camp from the upper level of the Boat House. Oak was responsible for water safety during the afternoon swimming period, but he would have been unaware if even a dozen swimmers were calling for help.

Finally, on Thursday he saw the signal. With lights out at sundown around 9 p.m., we agreed that an 11 p.m. rendezvous would be safe. We were to meet on the shore at the northern boundary of the girls camp where the bank had eroded, forming a natural ramp leading down to the water's edge. This spot was 200 or 300 hundred yards from the nearest Four-Way building and well screened by cedars. Oak and I would canoe without a light for fear that a flash of light from the lake would be seen on shore. The girls had a flashlight and would signal their location when they heard us approach.

To prepare for our escapade, we had placed a canoe and paddles in a cedar thicket at the south end of the Hayo-Went-Ha beach. A path between the camp buildings on the lower level and the New Lodge on the level above passed within 10 yards of the canoe. There was a clump of white birches marking the point we could leave the path and reach the canoe.

We executed the first part of our plan without a hitch. We left our respective cabins without disturbing any campers and made our way along the path to the birches. We had not expected the night to be so dark, but it was the time of the new moon. We stumbled in the dark until we spotted the glimmering birches. We put the canoe in without a sound and carefully paddled the canoe toward the rendezvous.

SUMMER ROMANCE

The night was spectacular. There wasn't a cloud in the sky. The Milky Way had risen overhead above the trees and cast just enough starlight to silhouette the tree tops along the shore. It was reflected in a band of light on the lake.

In the early 1940s, the shoreline was almost unbroken cedars, creating a uniform blackness as we paddled slowly and scanned the shore. We paddled so quietly, and the shore was so dark we passed the rendezvous without noticing it or being seen by the girls. Overshooting our destination, we nearly hit the Four-Way swimming platform. A throaty alarm from me in the front of the canoe and noisy back paddling avoided a collision. It did not appear to disturb anyone at the girls camp, but the girls had heard it and were flashing their light as we turned the canoe around. A minute later we were beaching the canoe as quietly as we could.

Emboldened by the night and the adventure, as soon as I could be sure the dim form was Barbara and not Jane, I gave her a hug and a kiss. The kiss started off more as a bump but quickly turned into the real thing. But during the clench my glasses, knocked crooked by the bump, fell off. We spent the next few minutes on hands and knees patting the ground in the darkness, giggling while we searched for my glasses; the girls thought the flashlight might give us away. Once found, we had a whispered conversation about our respective efforts to sneak out of camp.

Oak and Jane, the leaders in this adventure, were more interested in making out than whispering and contributed less and less to the conversation. Barbara and I weren't so forward and sat on the bank admiring the stars. We were just beginning to share some kisses when we saw a light in the trees in the direction of the camp. Immediately as still as mice, we could hear two counselors conferring whether the noises had come from our direction. We froze for five long minutes until the light and voices faded away.

Oak and I were interested in resuming operations, but the girls were afraid there would be a bed check at camp. We agreed to use Oak's sister as an intermediary to find other occasions to meet whether on the lake or in Central Lake. With a last kiss and squeeze, the girls disappeared into the pitch-black woods, moving quietly toward camp. We promised to wait at least 15 minutes before launching the canoe and paddling back to camp.

Oak and I spent the 15 minutes reliving our adventure and romantic conquests in whispers. Then as silently as we could, we floated the canoe and set off to camp.

It was well after midnight when we reach the beach at Hayo-Went-Ha. As the canoe touched the beach, Cap's voice called out from the dark bank, "Oak, is that you and Keena? I expect to see you two young men at my cabin in the morning at reveille!" "Yes sir," Oak replied. There were no further directives from the bank and we quickly put the canoe away.

We huddled for a few minutes by the Boat House, planning the cover story we would tell Cap. We wondered why Cap had not confronted us on the beach and had it out with us then and there. We knew we would be in big trouble if the nature of our midnight trip was discovered. We speculated we would be demoted as counselors or perhaps sent home in disgrace.

As Oak and I conferred on a strategy for our meeting with Cap at dawn, we acknowledged the ideal Hayo-Went-Ha man should always tell the truth, but we agreed application of the ideal in this situation would be unwise. We decided our story would be we had heard fishing was better during the new moon. Cap had not met us at the canoe, so he would not know we had no fishing rods. Our lack of fish could be explained by our conclusion that the new moon fishing story was an old wives' tale; after all, it was true we had not had a single bite during our hour on the water.

Notwithstanding the adventure or Cap's discovery of our outing, I fell asleep as soon as I crept into my cabin. Reveille came early, and I was still half asleep when I emerged from the cabin and Oak ran up and grabbed my arm. He hauled me toward Cap's cabin and reminded me of our cover story. Cap seemed a little surprised as we approached because we should have been herding our campers down to the morning swim.

Oak took the lead. "Cap, you asked to see us last night and

here we are." Ever on the initiative, Oak continued, "The fishing was pretty poor."

With a puzzled look, Cap was about to ask what on earth Oak was talking about when someone called about a problem with the water pump. Faced with a genuine problem, Cap did not have time to ask what Oak meant. With a distracted look over his shoulder as he headed for the pump house, he said, "Well, I hope fishing is better next time." Oak and I could not believe our good luck. To our relief, Cap never returned to the subject.

We shared our story with the other counselors, several of whom seemed particularly interested in our encounter with Cap and how we had hoped to fool him about the real purpose of our midnight canoeing expedition. They were sure Cap would have seen through our cover story in a minute.

Despite my desperate hope and letters back and forth with Alice, Oak and I were unsuccessful in arranging further meetings with Jane and Barbara.

The girls camp ended that summer a few days after Hayo-Went-Ha. I stayed on to help close camp. I was in Central Lake with Clarence and the camp truck on errands the day the girls caught the train home. Coming out of Bachmann's, I realized the girls were two blocks away at the train station. I hurried down, hoping to meet Barbara. I caught up with her as the girls were boarding the train. There was not time and it was not the place for a quick kiss and a hug. There was just time to exchange addresses and promises to write before she was the last girl on the platform and the conductor was impatiently calling "All Aboard" the third time. So, I waited on the platform, she leaned out of the window, and we waved to each other as the train left for Traverse City.

On the train ride to Detroit after camp ended, Oak and I were sitting together, reliving our after-hours visit to the girls camp. Suddenly Cap's voice boomed out behind us, "Oak, is that you and Keena? I expect to see you two young men at my cabin in the morning at reveille!" Then another voice squeaked out "Oooh, yes sir," followed by a great deal of laughter.

The voice belonged to Harry Speelman, one of the senior counselors who had captained Michigan State's football team. He had learned to mimic Cap's voice perfectly, which I used to good effect in a theatrical sketch the following summer.

Oak had been unable to keep our planned rendezvous with Jane and Barbara secret. Harry and another counselor had silently followed us down to the canoe and waited patiently in the dark to give us a good scare on our return. Their plan was shared with most counselors. A surprising number were nearby at reveille hoping to see first hand our adventure exposed under cross examination by Cap. They had had a lot of laughs among themselves as we boasted later of fooling Cap with our fishing story.

Barb and I wrote to each other in the fall and winter of 1941. I struggled at Fountain Valley and her letters were a great help. I hoped to see her in the summer of 1942, but the war changed many plans. She did not return to Four-Way Lodge in 1942 and our letters had stopped by the time I enlisted in October.

SUMMER ROMANCE

Four-Way Lodge Girls[B]

Barbara

TORCH LAKE SUMMERS

CHAPTER ELEVEN

WINTER OF DISCONTENT

The summer of 1941 had begun with an argument with my mother about returning to Fountain Valley for my senior year that was unresolved when I left for Hayo-Went-Ha. It resumed on my return from camp in late August. Again, over my objection, I was dispatched to Fountain Valley.

My drums stayed home. They had been too much of a distraction. After a second summer with our camp trio, I decided to branch out and learn the trumpet. My mother agreed to support trumpet lessons at Fountain Valley. On the bright side, my Grosse Pointe friend Russ Nutter would finish high school at Fountain Valley, so I would have a friend from home to keep me company.

The fall semester started well enough. I applied myself, the price I had to pay to take part in the fall play. As a senior, I auditioned for and won the part of the Stage Manager in the fall production of Thornton Wilder's *Our Town*. *Our Town* had opened on Broadway in 1938. I learned later that we were one of the first student productions. I relished the part and think I mostly carried it off. That production cemented my lifelong love of and devotion to the theater. My role in the fall play did much to help me through the first two months at Fountain Valley.

But, when the play ended in late October, I had had enough and told my mother I was coming home unless she shipped me my drum set. My mother consulted a child psychiatrist who advised her to send the drum set, so she did.

Between Grosse Pointe, camp, and Fountain Valley, I had little interest in the turmoil in Europe. December 7, 1941, changed that. School seemed even more inconsequential once the United States declared war. I was a history buff and had a rose-colored view of war, as do most who have not encountered the beast in the flesh. My disaffection with school, my interest in military history, and my strong sense of patriotism engendered by the Pearl Harbor attack, combined to make me eager to join the army. I expressed that sentiment on arriving home for Christmas in 1941 to my mother's dismay. A woman of strong principle, she understood and supported America's entry into the war. But it was another thing to hear her 17-year-old son's intention to enlist. I wanted to drop out of Fountain Valley and enlist when home.

My mother sent me to the psychiatrist she had consulted in the fall. He interviewed me and then advised my mother I would be better off at home. That settled it. I would not have to return to Fountain Valley after Christmas and I could finish high school in Grosse Pointe.

In fairness to Fountain Valley, the problem with my academic career was me, not the school. After I was discharged from the Army in 1946, I needed a recommendation to get into Colorado College. I wrote the headmaster, pleading, "Although you may not feel qualified to give me a scholastic recommendation [an understatement], I am sure a character reference would be a very great help." The tactful reference sent to Colorado College described me as a "Fine, reliable young man with a special talent in dramatics."

My last semester in high school is best remembered as five months of agonized waiting. The only high point was, as you might expect, the Pointe Players' spring production, *Tovarich*, a comedy in three acts. The plot involves a White Russian family reduced to domestic service in Paris after the Revolution. I played Commissar Goratchenko. Although I was proud of it, I suspect I brought to the stage the worst Russian accent ever attempted. When the play ended, I could not wait to turn 18 on July 5, 1942.

My school year ended without a graduation; I was two semesters behind in required courses. I did not complete my high school requirements and receive a high school diploma until I returned to Grosse Pointe after the war.

As the school year drew to a close in Grosse Pointe, the suspended argument with my mother resumed. She felt I would be too young in my 18th summer to become a soldier and thought me too small to boot. Further, in August 1941, I promised Cap to return for one more summer as a counselor, a prospect I had looked forward to until Pearl Harbor.

So, one more accommodation was achieved between the battling parties. I would honor my commitment to Hay-Went-Ha but then could enlist if that was still how I felt in the fall.

CHAPTER TWELVE

THEATER AT CAMP

Although I loved Hayo-Went-Ha, I did not look forward to my last summer at camp. I was looking past the summer to enlistment in the fall. I was very disappointed Barbara was not returning to Four-Way Lodge which I had learned from a letter in May. What saved the summer of 1942 at Hayo-Went-Ha was theater.

I wrote Cap in April 1942, proposing that one of my duties in the coming summer would be leading a drama program. If I was committed to limbo for the summer, I was determined to spend it on what I loved if I could. I described with pride and a certain amount of exaggeration my career on stage. While I am sure Cap discounted some of my theater resume as boasting, he knew me well and promptly wrote back, supporting my proposal. While the annual end-of-season talent show had often featured short skits, they were written and produced by the campers, and memorable for nothing other than their tom foolery. I expect Cap hoped for a pleasant change.

The venue was the New Lodge, dedicated in 1930. The main room was large enough for all the campers and staff to gather. At one end of the room is a massive stone fireplace with rocks gathered from the U.P. and, at the other, a small recessed stage. During my third year at camp the moose antlers now over the proscenium where brought to camp by campers returning from a Canadian trip. That made quite a story around the campfire.

I tried my hand at two pieces of theater that summer. Because I was familiar with *Our Town*, I chose to produce Act 1. Act 1 has a variety of parts and only Stage Manager's part was daunting. I consulted with Cap about the threatening copyright language in the front of my script, but we concluded that it could not apply to a one-night production in the backwoods of northern Michigan.

I was lucky that Rafe Merrill had had a high school drama class and was up to the challenge of learning Stage Manager's long lines. The play has simple staging instructions; the set is an open stage and there are few props. However, we took a few liberties and painted a backdrop showing the roof tops and church steeples of Grover's Corners and added a few physical props not called for in the script. The cast enjoyed acting out the rest of the props as envisioned by the script and its stage directions. With help from Miss Edna, Cap's wife, we cobbled costumes together out of whatever campers had brought to camp.

It turned out to be a lot harder to direct others than to learn my own lines. But, the production was as much of a success as it could have been. We performed the play the last week of July. Cap was complimentary, and the cast and crew had a good time.

What I enjoyed most, however, was my other theatrical production, a skit for talent night based on another drama about a sorcerer, *The Sorcerer's Apprentice*. Disney released *Fantasia*, including *The Sorcerer's Apprentice* as one of its animated shorts, in 1940. I saw it twice over Christmas break that year.

I thought it would be fun to do a skit with six parts — the sorcerer, his apprentice, and four magic brooms. I took the role of apprentice and based the character on Ben Harmon who had been given the responsibility for rebuilding a retaining wall by the Boat House, a project that had gone on in fits and starts all summer. Ben was a good friend who had several very recognizable catch phrases he repeated over and over that summer. I incorporated them into my persona as the sorcerer's apprentice.

I cast the campers who helped Ben as the brooms. Their activities in the skit were based loosely on all the difficulties Ben faced on his summer project. It was the campers/brooms who did everything wrong, complicating the project and multiplying the work.

The sorcerer, of course, was a thinly-disguised version of Cap played by Harry Speelman.

I made up for the simplicity of the *Our Town* staging in my production of the *Apprentice*. With help from Clarence and campers in the workshop, I developed a outthrust from the stage. It permitted me to locate upward facing stage lights in the floor. Miss Edna helped me make semi-transparent sorcery gowns for the sorcerer and his assistant. Art Townsend, my lighting crew, turned the upward-facing lights on whenever the sorcerer or apprentice cast a spell. Casting a spell, besides an incantation invoking the spirit of Hayo-Went-Ha, required a certain swirling of the gown that, by virtue of the under-lighting, had a great visual effect.

The skit ended with the brooms whirling madly around, shouting, banging buckets, and throwing water. As I spluttered and waved my wand helplessly, the sorcerer reappeared to save the day. We had rigged a flashlight beneath Harry's face, casting it in harsh and threatening shadows, creating a wonderfully sinister effect. The sorcerer leapt on stage and Harry, in this best imitation of Cap's voice, demanded "What goes on here, you saucy varlet?!?" At that, the light under my gown went out and my wand fell apart. The skit closed with the sorcerer admonishing his apprentice and the four brooms, "Remember, Each for All and All for Each."

New Lodge Stage[HWH]

CHAPTER THIRTEEN
CAMP AND CHILDHOOD END

I was a cauldron of emotions after the campers left in August 1942. I stayed on with the other counselors to close up the camp — closing up the tents and cabins, finding the odds and ends left behind, and putting boats and equipment away. We were experienced counselors and had been through the drill of closing up camp several times. We knew where everything was stored and how to secure the boats and equipment so they would be ready for use the next summer. Yet, unlike past summers when Cap trusted us to close most of the camp with little supervision, he spent each day with us, lifting, packing, cleaning, closing.

Cap knew what the fall would bring for me and the other older counselors who would enlist at summer's end. Several former campers and counselors were already in the armed services, but the camp had not yet had its first casualty. Cap dreaded that day and was particularly patient and encouraging with us. He had had cousins and neighbors injured or killed in the First World War and had no delusions about what was to come.

Each night that last week we spent around a campfire

fire, telling stories and singing camp songs late into the night. As each night ended, we sang "Hey, Hey, Hey, Hayo-Went-Ha" from our first Hayo-Went-Ha campfire.

> A campfire dies; another lights again
> Alive with memories that sing in the wind.
> And I know where I'm going 'cause I know where
>   I've been.
> And, it's hey, hey, hey, Hayo-Went-Ha.
>
> And it's here I want to be one summer more,
> On Hayo-Went-Ha's hills and trails by the shore,
> Where three brothers walked 30 years before,
> And others will walk 100 years more,
> And I'm here because I know what I'm walking for.
> And it's hey, hey, hey, Hayo-Went-Ha.

Cap had no special stories or words of wisdom around those campfires. In his eyes, at work, at play, at peace, at war, the principles were the same: a strong faith, leadership from the front, and, as trite as it might seem to an outsider because of its frequent repetition (but never was to any of us), "Each for all and all for each."

On the last evening, as we huddled together on the train platform in Central Lake, Cap told us we would be called to face difficult times but if we were true to "each for all and all for each," our men (he expected us to be leaders of men) would follow us through the worst of times. His confidence in me did much to dispel the gnawing fear of what I had committed to do — to serve at the risk of my life, in a place far away, in a cause looking in the late summer of 1942 just short of hopeless.

The last train trip from Central Lake for the nine of us senior counselors was an odd affair — boisterous then quiet, then boisterous again. Our attention was so fragmented that after twenty minutes of bridge, we threw our hands in and told camp stories. Then conversation changed to the future which approached like a dense squall coming down the lake — an artificial brightness ahead of the impenetrable gray wall of rain

CAMP AND CHILDHOOD END

and wind. But, unlike the times at camp when we sailed to safety on shore, now we were about to launch our boats and head into the storm. I was enlisting in just a few weeks as were Tommy Baldwin and two of the other counselors. The other five knew enlistment or the draft would follow soon after their 18th birthdays. Despite brave talk in the press of a short war for America like World War One, we sensed that would not be the case. Because the prospect was too awful to discuss for long stretches, conversation returned to camp stories, only to shift inevitably to what lay before us.

In Grand Rapids, the conductor roused us a little after midnight, and five of the boys, headed mostly to the Chicago area, left the train. Our goodbyes were muted — a last Tigers versus White Sox baseball insult and then a "See you." No promises of meeting again — that wasn't the world of August 1942 for boys headed for war.

In the early 1950s on a buying trip to New York, I met one of the Chicago counselors on that train trip. We did a simultaneous double take as we passed each other on Second Avenue. We chatted for a while and had a drink. Neither of us knew what had happened to the other four Chicago boys who left the train with him in Grand Rapids; they had disappeared into the gray squall of war we had seen coming.

The four of us remaining on the train headed for Detroit — Tommy Baldwin, Jerry Greenwood, Ben Harmon and me — dozed and talked quietly as the train traveled east. There were several delays for unknown reasons, with the train halted in the middle of nowhere; no explanation given — or asked. We were in no rush. Our ninth and last round trip together was nearly over. We would leave our childhood behind when we stepped off the train in Detroit.

We finally arrived at the Michigan Central station in Detroit at 12:30 p.m. on Friday, August 21. Jerry's and Ben's fathers were there to meet them. We made small talk for a few minutes, shook hands and again it was "See you." No goodbyes.

My tradition with Uncle Jere had fallen by the wayside. Because his health had declined, he could no longer meet me and take me to lunch and the ball game. Now I visited him after my first day home, to relive the summer while sitting in the garden at Stonedge, his home on Provencal in Grosse Pointe Farms.

Tommy Baldwin lived in Dearborn and, as usual, he would lug his trunk to Michigan Avenue and catch a streetcar home. But that Friday, neither of us was prepared to part company as we left the station. There was a discussion about leaving our trunks with a porter and walking two blocks to Briggs Stadium where the Saint Louis Browns were playing the Tigers. If we moved briskly, we could see the first pitch. It was a sunny afternoon and there was a small crowd milling around on Michigan Avenue. After some debate, that's what we did.

I had received a note from my mother asking me to call when I arrived, and she would send someone to fetch me. I called home and left word I had arrived safely and would make my way home by bus.

Tommy and I had the stadium mostly to ourselves. I bet attendance was less than 5,000. Tommy was a big fan of Hal White, the Tiger's starter in that game. We found seats in the lower deck behind home plate where we could watch his pitches curve across the plate. After the third inning we moved around to the third base side to sit in the sun. I knew Uncle Jere's box would be empty and over the years I had become friends with the ushers who served those box seats. To them, Tommy and I were Mr. Hutchins' guests for the afternoon.

We sat in Uncle Jere's box seats just inside third, in the 4th row back from the field. I told Tommy about the great games I had watched from those seats. I had even caught a foul ball once. That afternoon, White pitched a complete game and the Tigers won, 4 to 1. I wasn't sure if I would ever sit with Uncle Jere in that box again, and I did not — he died in 1943 while I was in the army.

When the game ended, there was nothing left to do but make our way out of the ballpark, collect our trunks at the Michigan Central station, and stand awkwardly together on

Michigan Avenue, Tommy headed west and me headed east. There wasn't much left to say and, after we stood on the curb for a few minutes, a westbound streetcar saved us continuing embarrassment. As Tommy boarded the streetcar, it was a quick handshake and a "See you." Then, as he was on the top step, "Keep the flame burning until we meet again."

I crossed the street and took a bus home to join my family, spend time with Uncle Jere, and visit friends. The next two months were just a restless time of hellos and goodbyes. I enlisted in mid October.

Tommy died on July 10, 1943, the second day of the invasion of Sicily, the hardest one to lose of all my Hayo-Went-Ha friends. By that time, childhood was long gone and Hayo-Went-Ha far away.

THE END

FAREWELL.

CAMP AND CHILDHOOD END

Dave Keena, U.S. Army, 1942[A]

TORCH LAKE SUMMERS

ACKNOWLEDGEMENTS

My inspirations to write Dave Keena's story were several. First, three long-time Hayo-Went-Ha campers and counselors I am pleased to call friends — in order of acquaintance, Dave Martin, Steve Foley, and Jim Austin. In those guys I have come to admire how the lessons learned at Hayo-Went-Ha play out in life.

My second inspiration was getting to know something about Hayo-Went-Ha beyond the Boat House visible from our cottage dock. Over the last four years, Jim, Dave, and Steve have introduced me to Hayo-Went-Ha lore. My previous contact was limited to listening to the camp bugler sound "Taps" summer evenings. I like very much what I have heard from them. That led me to an interest in Hayo-Went-Ha history, satisfied by K. Patrick Rode's book *On the Sloping Pine Hills* (Cincinnati: The Merten Company, 2003). I have interviewed Pat and he has shared camp lore with me.

My final inspiration came when I took my wife Ginger and her sister Lucy to the K Patrick Rode Dining Hall to find their father in the pictures on its walls. After a lot of peering and guessing, they found him in one framed photo. Driving back to the cottage from the visit, I decided it was time finally to write the story of Dave Keena's summers at camp.

This story would not be possible without Pat's history of Cap Drury's years at Hayo-Went-Ha and the stories Pat shared with me. I believe Pat feels, as I do, there is value in telling the Hayo-Went-Ha story from a camper's point of view. He has most generously given me permission to lean, very heavily in some places, on material and photos in his book and on the stories he told me.

Although many of the adventures in this memoir are taken from the pages of Pat's book, Dave Keena, unlike Forrest Gump, did not participate in all of them. I have tried to be as true as any story teller ever is to facts and dates. I am confident Pat, as the teller of many tales around

Hayo-Went-Ha campfires, appreciates the demands the art of storytelling place on the literal truth. Any deviations are attributable either to my error or the demands of the tale. I hope this story does credit to Hayo-Went-Ha, to Cap, and to Pat.

Fountain Valley School of Colorado generously provided me a copy of Dave's high school file, photos of the school, and photos from the 1940/41 and 1941/42 yearbooks. That led to insights into Dave as a teenager and provided a background to his years at camp.

This memoir was possible only with the help of others. My thanks to Director Dave Martin for permission to copy and use photographs from the walls of the K Patrick Rode Dining Hall. Rob Wilkinson, a camp alumni, has generously created the illustration for the book. Jeanette Gillespie, who created the cover art and book layout, is another of the wonderful people I have been fortunate to meet through Hayo-Went-Ha. Special thanks to Rose Bechtold, whose beautiful photographs of the Chain of Lakes grace many walls in northwest Michigan, for providing the cover photo showing off the blues of Torch Lake. I am indebted to Mary Kay and Ed McDuffie's wonderful book, *Torch Lake: The History of Was-Wah-Go-Ning* (Megissee County Publications 2009), for the details of Antrim County and Torch Lake in the 1930s. I thank Uncle Jere for telling me his story (from beyond the grave) via *Jere C. Hutchins, A Personal Story* (Detroit 1938). Friends Jim Smith and Peggy Ptaznick provided meaningful editorial comments on my draft. Special thanks to the proprietress of Bachmann's Store for the story of the long sled ride down Dean's Hill, through the village of Central Lake and across the bridge. On my visits to Bachmann's today, so little changed from the 1940s, I have visions of campers in short pants spending their last dime on candy before boarding the train for home at the end of the summer. And finally, an apology to the memory of Bob Thurston for attributing his song, "Hey, Hey, Hey, Hayo-Went-Ha," to an unknown songwriter in the 1930s.

Details of Dave and his family appear in this memoir courtesy of family stories provided by my wife Ginger and

ACKNOWLEDGEMENTS

my historical research. Cap and Edna Drury, Nurse Vail, Clarence Hansen and Harry Speelman are taken from life — more accurately, from *On the Sloping Pine Hills*. The boys who shared summers with Dave are mostly lost to history, all but their names painted on the timbers of the Boat House. The campers and counselors who accompany Dave in this story are fictional and stand imperfectly in their stead.

Dave Keena has been gone 30 years. I hope weaving information from Hayo-Went-Ha, Fountain Valley School and family stories about Dave, embroidered with what is true of most adolescent boys, will bring a little of him back to his family and me.

Craig Hupp, May 2018

TORCH LAKE SUMMERS

PHOTO CREDITS

SOURCE CODE	SOURCE
A	Author
B	Bentley Historical Library, Four-Way Lodge, a camp for girls on Torch Lake Michigan (1937), p. 8
DPL	Detroit Public Library, NAHC, Lazarnick Collection, image na019883
FVS	Fountain Valley School of Colorado
GPS	Grosse Pointe South High School
HWH	Camp Hayo-Went-Ha
JCH	*Jere C. Hutchins - A Personal Story*
MSU	Plymouth District Library: Charles Draper Collection, Plymouth Historical Museum, (Item #JKR03f005); Helena District Library: Postcard Collection, Helena Twp. Historical Museum, Alden, MI (Items # CE01a112 and #CE01a038) available on MSU, Making of Modern Michigan, http://mmm.lib.msu.edu/
RB	Rose Bechtold
ULS	University Liggett School
PG	pedalgood.com

Made in the USA
Middletown, DE
12 July 2019